The Fairy Tales of Charles Perrault

Angela Carter (1940–1992) published her first novel, *Shadow Dance*, in 1966 and was immediately recognized as one of Britain's most original writers. Eight other novels followed, as well as four collections of stories, a book of essays, two collections of journalism, and a volume of radio plays. In addition to translating the fairy tales of Charles Perrault, she edited collections of fairy and folk tales as well as *Wayward Girls & Wicked Women: An Anthology of Subversive Stories*. From 1976 through 1978 she was Arts Council of Great Britain Fellow in Creative Writing at Sheffield University, and in 1980 and 1981 she was a visiting professor in the writing program at Brown University. She traveled and taught widely in the United States and Australia but lived in London.

Charles Perrault (1628–1703) was a civil servant and a member of L'Académie française engaged in the literary affairs of his day. His fairy tales were first published under a pseudonym in 1697. Whether originally intended for adults or children, these tales have been loved by children through hundreds of translations and retellings, and perhaps thousands of artists' interpretations.

Jack Zipes is a professor of German at the University of Minnesota. A specialist in folklore, fairy tales, and children's literature, he has translated such works as the fairy tales of the Brothers Grimm and Hermann Hess, written several books of criticism, and edited numerous anthologies, including *Spells of Enchantment: The Wondrous Fairy Tales of Western Culture* (Penguin). For Penguin Classics he has edited *The Wonderful World of Oz*, *Pinocchio*, and *Peter Pan*. He has been honoured with the Distinguished Scholar Award by the International Association for the Fantastic in the Arts.

ANGELA CARTER

The Fairy Tales of Charles Perrault

Introduction by JACK ZIPES

PENGUIN BOOKS

PENGUIN CLASSICS

Published by the Penguin Group
Penguin Books Ltd, 80 Strand, London WC2R ORL, England
Penguin Group (USA) Inc., 375 Hudson Street, New York, New York 10014, USA
Penguin Group (Canada), 90 Eglinton Avenue East, Suite 700, Toronto, Ontario, Canada M4P 2Y3
(a division of Pearson Penguin Canada Inc.)
Penguin Ireland, 25 St Stephen's Green, Dublin 2, Ireland (a division of Penguin Books Ltd)
Penguin Group (Australia), 250 Camberwell Road, Camberwell, Victoria 3124, Australia
(a division of Pearson Australia Group Pty Ltd)
Penguin Books India Pvt Ltd, 11 Community Centre, Panchsheel Park, New Delhi – 110 017, India
Penguin Group (NZ), 67 Apollo Drive, Rosedale, North Shore 0632, New Zealand
(a division of Pearson New Zealand Ltd)
Penguin Books (South Africa) (Pty) Ltd, 24 Sturdee Avenue, Rosebank,
Johannesburg 2196, South Africa

Penguin Books Ltd, Registered Offices: 80 Strand, London WC2R ORL, England

www.penguin.com

First published in Great Britain under the current title by Victor Gollancz 1977
First published in the United States of America by Avon Books 1979
This edition published in the United States of America as *Little Red Riding Hood, Cinderella, and Other Classic Fairy Tales of Charles Perrault* 2008
Published as *The Fairy Tales of Charles Perrault* in Penguin Classics 2008

3

Printed in England by Clays Ltd, St Ives plc

978-0-141-18995-6

www.greenpenguin.co.uk

Contents

Introduction

THE REMAKING OF CHARLES PERRAULT AND HIS FAIRY TALES

Very few critics realize that Charles Perrault played a highly significant role in Angela Carter's development as a fairy-tale writer. If it were not for the fact that she was commissioned to translate Perrault's *Histoires ou contes du temps passé avec des moralités* (1697) in 1976, she would probably not have conceived her unique, groundbreaking collection of feminist fairy tales, *The Bloody Chamber and Other Stories,* published in 1979. To be sure, her own stories turn Perrault's tales inside out in defiant and definitive ways. Perrault may have been her "fairy godfather," but Carter did not accept his "magical" gifts as a docile obedient goddaughter. She was an unruly, mischievous "child," and many of her own fairy tales were subversive renditions of his classical tales. In fact, one could possibly argue that even her translations of Perrault's tales were an unusual brazen appropriation of his works, and that she remade Perrault and his tales into something different from what they were. This was typical of Carter, a very independent and original thinker, who rebelled against classical tradition while absorbing and re-creating it in her own distinct down-to-earth, baroque manner.

Carter was born Angela Olive Stalker on May 7, 1940, in Eastbourne, Sussex, and soon after her birth, she was evacuated with her brother to South Yorkshire to live with her maternal grandmother so that her family could avoid the bombing of London during the war years. Her mother, Olive (Farthing) Stalker, accompanied the children while her father, Hugh Stalker, a journalist, remained in London for most of this period. At the end of the war, the family was reunited in London, where Carter, as she would later say in numerous interviews, spent a happy childhood but developed a stormy relationship with her mother and suffered from anorexia as a teenager. She was strongly influenced by her grandmother, a confident and candid woman with leftist political views. Her mother, on the other hand, tended to be more proper and set ambitious goals for her daughter. When Carter graduated high school in 1959, she did not have the grades that warranted a scholarship to the university. So her father helped her find an apprentice position as a journalist for the *Croydon Advertiser.* It was during this time that she met Paul Carter, a chemist, whom she married at age twenty. Carter always insisted that she had married to get away from her family, and indeed, she moved with him to Bristol, where she enrolled at the university in the English Department with a major in medieval literature. Her studies of medieval literature led her to take a great interest in romances with fairy-tale motifs and in poems and plays that were part of an ornate fey tradition from Spenser and Shakespeare up through the British romantics Keats and Coleridge. In addition, Carter became part of folk music circles with her husband and toured the festivals in Great Britain. While working toward her degree she often attended the cinema, taking a great interest in the French nouvelle vague, especially in the films by Godard and Truffaut, and began writing fiction. After completing her studies in 1966, she focused on her own creative writing and published her first novel, *Shadow Dance* (1966), that reflected the turbulent sixties at British universities. It was followed quickly by two other novels, *The Magic Toyshop* (1967) and *Several Perceptions* (1968); both works were explorations of sexual fantasies and employed fairy-tale motifs in unusual ways to test the limits of realism. *Several Perceptions* won the Somerset Maugham Award, and she decided to use the prize money to travel across America. It was a very critical period for Carter, and she later stated: "I can date to that time and to that sense of heightened awareness of the society around me in the summer of 1968 my own questioning of the nature of my reality as a woman. How that social fiction of my 'feminity' was created, by means outside my control, and palmed off on me as the real thing."

While in America, Carter and her husband decided to separate, and she went off to live and work in Japan for three years. It is unclear exactly what she did while she was in Japan. Some biographers have asserted that she left California to join a lover in Japan and that she had odd jobs as a teacher, editor, and waitress while living there. Whatever the case may be, Carter did not abandon her writing. She finished *Heroes and Villains* (1969), a kind of science-fiction gothic novel in which the protagonist, Marianne, abandons a city of professors and scientists to live in the wilderness with a barbarian tribe. She also used this time to experiment with shorter fiction and sent some stories to be published in magazines in the UK. Interestingly, she wrote two highly original avant-garde fairy tales for children, *The Donkey Prince* (1970) and *Miss Z, the Dark Young Lady* (1970), which anticipated her translations of Perrault and her own feminist fairy tales in *The Bloody Chamber.*

By the time Carter returned to England in 1972, she had become more certain of her craft as an experimental writer, and she had become more independent in her personal life. She divorced Paul Carter in 1972 and moved to Spa, where she made her home until 1977. Quite often she worked on many diverse projects at the same time, partially because she had to support herself as a freelance writer, and partially because she had such broad interests and felt deep political commitments to the feminist movement and to leftist causes. In 1974 she published her first collection of short stories, *Fireworks,* many of which had been written in Japan and had already been published in small magazines. In 1975 she began contributing articles to the journal *New Society,* and it was at about this time that she agreed to translate Perrault's fairy tales, which she finished in 1977.

As she began her work on Perrault, she also started writing her own original stories that formed the basis of *The Bloody Chamber.* Some of them were published in the new avant-garde magazine *Bananas,* founded in 1975 and edited by Emma Tennant. Thanks to Tennant's encouragement, Carter and other writers such as Michèle Roberts and Sara Maitland could give free rein to their imaginations, and they wrote several feminist fairy tales that were published in *Bananas* during the late 1970s. Carter herself was now in one of her most creative phases, experimenting in diverse forms of fiction and nonfiction. Aside from her more prosaic Perrault translations, her most important innovative projects were the novel *The Passion of New Eve* (1977), the long essay *The Sadeian Woman* (1979), and her collection of unique feminist fairy tales, *The Bloody Chamber* (1979), which enabled her to transcend the limits of translation. The novel depicts a male protagonist named Evelyn, who comes to a futuristic New York only to experience maddening adventures of sexual transformation as Eve that sets him/her on a voyage further west to a new kind of Eden. *The Sadeian Woman* was—and perhaps still is—a highly controversial analysis of sadomasochism and sexual relations between men and women. Using the Marquis de Sade's novels, Carter argued that women, especially feminists, too often begin with the assumption that they are victims and have little agency in their lives. Instead of victimization she focused more on how women could realize their deep sexual desires, whether sadistic or masochistic, and could determine their sexual and social roles with greater freedom. Much of the philosophy in *The Sadeian Woman* is fully developed in *The Bloody Chamber*, in which classical tales, such as "Bluebeard," "Cinderella," "Little Red Riding Hood," "Beauty and the Beast," and "Puss in Boots," are given unusual twists that open up the possibilities for sexual play and social transformation. At the very least, the tales are feminist provocations written in a terse metaphorical language that is often stunning.

In 1977 Carter moved to London with her partner, Mark Pearce, whom she married shortly before her death, and she would make South London her home until she died in 1992. Her arrival in London virtually marked her arrival as one of the foremost British writers of magic realism and gothic fiction in the twentieth century. It also marked the beginning of the most productive period of her life, the period that revealed how multitalented she was as a writer. Aside from producing two intriguing picaresque novels, *Nights at the Circus* (1984) and *Wise Children* (1991), both filled with fantastic motifs and unusual plots and wordplay, Carter gave talks and taught courses on creative writing at universities in England, Australia, and America. She wrote numerous articles for *The Guardian, The Independent,* and *New Statesman* that were collected in two volumes of her journalism, *Nothing Sacred* (1982) and *Expletives Deleted* (1992). Her book *Black Venus* (1985), also known as *Saints and Strangers,* through its fictionalized portraits of historical characters, questioned traditional historical assumptions and views. She also participated in writing the screenplays for the film *The Company of Wolves* (1984), based on her marvelous rendition of "Little Red Riding Hood," and for the cinematic adaptation of *The Magic Toyshop* (1987). At the same time she wrote plays for radio based on some of her short stories and two original pieces on Richard Dadd and Ronald Firbank. Some of her other projects, such as a libretto for an opera of Virginia Woolf's *Orlando,* were never realized. Nevertheless, all her unpublished writings that have appeared since her death show that she had a strong interest in writing for the media and for the theater. More important, perhaps, is that her interest in fairy tales never wavered throughout the period 1977–92. In fact, Carter wrote more books for children with fairy-tale themes, *Comic and Curious Cats* (1979), *The Music People* (1980), and *Moonshadow* (1982), and edited two important collections for adults, *The Virago Book of Fairy Tales* (also known as *The Old Wives' Fairy Tale Book,* 1990) and *The Second Virago Book of Fairy Tales* (also known as *Strange Things Still Sometimes Happen: Fairy Tales from around the World,* 1992). The depth and breadth of her knowledge was extraordinary for a writer who had never studied folklore at a university, and in many ways she "magically" transformed the genre, bringing it to new heights in the name of the folk, and especially in the name of feminism.

When Carter died of cancer in 1992, the novelist Salman Rushdie commented, "English literature has lost its high sorceress, its benevolent witch queen," and Margaret Atwood, the Canadian writer known for her rewriting of fairy tales, stated, "The amazing thing about her, for me, was that someone who looked so much like the Fairy Godmother . . . should actually be so much like the Fairy Godmother. She was the opposite of parochial. Nothing, for her, was outside the pale: she wanted to know about everything and everyone, and every place and every word. She reveled life and language hugely, and reveled in the diverse." Certainly, it is not strange that two of the finest contemporary novelists should use fairy-tale metaphors to describe Carter, who was devoted to changing the very nature of the fairy tale in radical ways. What is strange, however, is Carter's attraction to Charles Perrault, a well-born, conservative writer at Louis XIV's court, whose understanding of women and their social roles was very limited, to say the least.

Charles Perrault was born in 1628 into one of the more distinguished bourgeois families of Paris and grew up during the reign of Louis XIV. His father, Pierre Perrault, was a lawyer and member of the Paris Parliament, and his three living brothers—he was the youngest and brother of a twin who died six months after childbirth—all went on to become renowned in such fields as architecture, medicine, and law. In 1637 Perrault began studying at the Collège de Beauvais (near the Sorbonne), and at the age of fifteen he stopped attending school and largely taught himself all he needed to know so he could later take his law examinations. Perrault had been a brilliant student and rebelled against the narrow-minded manner in which philosophy was being taught at his school. In addition, he began writing and publishing burlesques with his friend Beaurain and his older brothers, Claude, Pierre, and Nicolas, and steeping himself in classical literature, philosophy, and religion.

During the 1640s Perrault took an interest in Jansenism and the popular political movement against King Louis XIV, and his early poetry demonstrated some favor for the Jansenists and the bourgeois opposition to the crown. Many intellectuals such as Pascal and Racine had been attracted to Jansenism, a branch of Catholic thought that emphasized predestination and was close to Calvinism. The Jansenist movement, however, was condemned by Pope Urban VIII in 1642, and Louis the XIV constantly oppressed the Jansenists in favor of the more traditional Jesuits. Although Perrault admired the moral fervor and thinking of the Jansenists, he soon became fearful about his support of Jansenism and gradually switched his position to support the king. In 1651 he passed the law examinations at the University of Orléans, and after working three years as a lawyer, he left the profession to become a secretary to his brother Pierre, who was the tax receiver of Paris.

Perrault, who had already published some minor poems, began taking more and more of an interest in literature rather than in assisting his brother. In 1659 he published two important poems, "Portrait d'Iris" and "Portrait de la Voix d'Iris," and by 1661 his public career as a poet was in full swing after he had published several poems celebrating the Peace of the Pyrenees, the marriage of Louis XIV, and the birth of the Dauphin. Perrault knew where his bread could best be buttered.

In 1663 he was appointed secretary to Jean-Baptiste Colbert, controller general of finances, perhaps the most influential minister in Louis XIV's government. For the next twenty years, until Colbert's death, Perrault, a workaholic, was able to accomplish a great deal in the arts and sciences due to Colbert's power and influence. In 1671 he was elected to the French Academy and was also placed in charge of the royal buildings—he was able to engage one of his brothers to help design the Louvre. While his primary duties as secretary entailed a great deal of attention to organizing events and administering Colbert's office, he continued writing poetry and took an active interest in cultural affairs of the court. In 1672 he married Marie Guichon, with whom he had three sons. She died in childbirth in 1678, and he never remarried, supervising the education of his children by himself.

When Colbert died in 1683, Perrault, who may have offended some powerful people at Louis XIV's court during the years he was under the protection of Colbert, was dismissed from government service. However, he had a pension and was able to support his family until his death. Released from governmental duties, Perrault could concentrate more on literary affairs, and in 1687, he helped inaugurate the "Quarrel of the Ancients and the Moderns" (*Parallèle des anciens et des modernes,* 1688–97) by reading a poem entitled "Le Siècle de Louis le Grand." Perrault took the side of modernism and believed that France and Christianity—here he sided with the Jansenists—could only make great progress and become like the great Greek and Roman empires of the past if the French writers and artists incorporated pagan beliefs and folklore into their sophisticated works and developed a culture of enlightenment. The point was not to imitate Greek and Roman culture but to become different if not unique. On the other hand, Nicolas Boileau, the poet and philosopher, and Jean Racine, the dramatist, took the opposite viewpoint and argued that France had to imitate the great empires of Greece and Rome and maintain stringent classical rules in respect to the arts. This literary quarrel, which had even greater cultural and political implications than just for the arts, lasted until 1697, at which time Louis XIV decided arbitrarily to end it in favor of Boileau and Racine. There was a truce, and Boileau and Perrault were reconciled. It was, however, an uneasy truce, and the "reconciliation" did not stop Perrault from trying to promote his ideas in his poetry and prose.

Perrault had always frequented the literary salons of his niece Mlle Marie-Jeanne Lhéritier, Mme Marie-Catherine d'Aulnoy, and other women, all talented writers, and was impressed if not influenced by the manner in which they were experimenting with fairy tales. He had also been annoyed by Boileau's satires written against women. Thus, without naming Boileau as his antagonist, he wrote three verse tales—"Griseldis" (1691), based on a story by Boccaccio, "Les Souhaits Ridicules" ("The Foolish Wishes," 1693), and "Peau d'Âne" ("Donkey Skin," 1694)—along with a long poem, *Apologie des femmes* (*The Vindication of Women*, 1694), in defense of women. Whether these works can be considered pro–women's rights today or poems in defense of women is another question. However, Perrault was definitely more progressive in regard to "the women question" than either Boileau or Racine, and his poems make use of a highly mannered style and folk motifs to stress the necessity of assuming an enlightened moral attitude toward women and exercising just authority.

By 1696, Perrault had embarked on a more ambitious project of transforming several popular folk tales with all their superstitious beliefs and magic into moralistic tales with an ironic rational style that would appeal to children and adults and demonstrate a modern approach to literature. His prose version of

"Sleeping Beauty" ("La Belle au Bois Dormant") was printed in the journal *Mercure Galant* in 1696, and in 1697 he published his famous collection of tales entitled *Histoires ou contes du temps passé,* which consisted of new versions of "Sleeping Beauty," "Little Red Riding Hood" ("Le Petit Chaperon Rouge"), "Blue Beard" ("Barbe Bleue"), "Cinderella" ("Cendrillon"), "Tom Thumb" ("Le Petit Poucet"), "Riquet with the Tuft" ("Riquet à la Houppe"), "Puss in Boots" ("Le Chat Botté"), and "The Fairies" ("Les Fées"). This book did not include his verse tales ("Griseldis," "The Foolish Wishes," and "Donkey Skin"), which were first included in a single volume in 1781. Almost all of these stories, with the possible exception of "Blue Beard," had circulated in an oral European tradition, and some versions had already been printed in the Italian collections of Giovan Francesco Straparola's *Le piacevoli notti* (*The Pleasant Nights,* 1550–53) and in Giambattista Basile's *Lo cunto de li cunti* (known in English as the *Pentamerone,* 1634–36).

Although *Histoires ou contes du temps passé* was published under the name of Pierre Perrault Darmancour, Perrault's son, and although some critics have asserted that the book was indeed written or at least coauthored by his son, the evidence has shown clearly that this could not have been the case, especially since his son had not published anything up to that point. Perrault, who had already prepublished some of the tales, was simply using his son's name to mask his own identity so that he would not be blamed for reigniting the Quarrel of the Ancients and the Moderns.

Some scholars have erroneously regarded Perrault's tales as written directly for children, but they overlook the fact that there was no children's literature per se at that time and that all the French writers, mainly women, were composing and reciting their fairy tales for their peers in the literary salons with veiled reference to conditions at Louis XIV's court. Clearly, Perrault intended them to make a final point in the Quarrel of the Ancients and the Moderns, and he obviously had an adult audience in mind that would understand his humor and the subtle manner in which he transformed folklore and widespread superstition to convey his position about the "modern" development of French civility. There are many intertextual references in his finely honed narratives that reveal how carefully Perrault composed the tales, referring subtly to La Fontaine, Boileau, Racine, and other prominent writers of this period, and was conscious of forging a new "modern" genre of writing. He had attended all the fairy-tale operas of Lully at King Louis XIV's court as well as many of the other magical extravaganzas; he interacted with almost all of the other innovative writers of fairy tales such as d'Aulnoy, Lhéritier, Catherine Bernard, Mlle de La Force, the chevalier de Mailly, Jean de Préchac, and Mme d'Auneuil and regarded himself as part of a "modern" vogue. When Perrault died in 1703, this vogue had become established as a literary genre, and the fairy tale thrived in France in the eighteenth century up to the time of the French Revolution, when Charles-Joseph Mayer published the forty-one volumes of fairy tales in his famous collection *Le cabinet des fées* (1785–89), which contained most of the tales published by various authors between 1695 and 1702. Of course, the genre of the literary fairy tale did not end with the outbreak of the French Revolution. Indeed, if anything, it continued to spread and grow more diverse and fascinating throughout the centuries.

There is no doubt that, among the writers of fairy tales during the 1690s, Perrault was the greatest stylist, which accounts for the fact that his tales have withstood the test of time. Furthermore, Perrault claimed that literature must become modern, and his transformation of folk motifs and literary themes into refined and provocative fairy tales still speak to the modern age, ironically in a way that may compel us to ponder whether the Age of Reason has led to the progress and happiness promised so charmingly in Perrault's tales.

To understand Perrault's fairy tales and their cultural ramifications up to the present, it is necessary to grasp the sociohistorical context in which the tales first appeared and the hidden debates and discourses in the tales themselves. For instance, Perrault's disagreements with Boileau about women's place in society were incorporated into the tales that he wrote from 1694 to 1697. If we include the verse tales with *Contes du temps passé*, there are eleven narratives altogether, and with the exception of "Riquet with the Tuft," "The Master Cat, or Puss in Boots," "Blue Beard," and "Little Thumbling," all the others ("Cinderella, or The Glass Slipper," "The Sleeping Beauty in the Woods," "Little Red Riding Hood," "Griseldis," "Donkey-Skin," "The Fairies," and "The Foolish Wishes") feature women, in particular, the comportment of women in desperate situations, and how their qualities enable them to triumph and find their proper place in society under masculine domination. Even "Ricky with the Tuft" and "Blue Beard" can be considered tales more concerned about women than men because the focus is on women who, when confronted with difficult choices, prove themselves to be valiant and noble despite maltreatment by powerful men. In fact, more than any of the important male writers of fairy tales before him, such as the Italians Giovan Francesco Straparola and Giambattista Basile, Perrault initiated a male discourse about gender relations that became foundational to the rise of the literary fairy tale as genre and cultural institution.

These "foundational" tales, or what we might call classical tales today, tend to reinforce patriarchal and patronizing notions of gender and power. Though the female characters are not mocked or parodied, Perrault wrote to illustrate what their "proper" place was in particular situations and how best to act in a civil way. This was also true for his male protagonists. In some respects, his fairy tales form a book on courtly manners based on Perrault's vision of how the course of the civilizing process should be directed. All his tales involve some sort of a learning process for both women and men so that they can establish their proper roles in society. For instance, Cinderella needs to demonstrate patience, humility, and industry to win a prince, whose basic function is to recognize her aristocratic virtues and to anoint her princess. In "Ricky with the Tuft" the princess must learn to alter her vision and see the world through an ugly man's eyes (also a powerful prince) if she is to remain an attractive, witty aristocrat. Her identity is virtually determined by the male gaze of Ricky. In "Little Red Riding Hood," a girl brings about her own rape and violent death because she does not know how to behave with dangerous seducers. In this case, the girl is punished because she is gullible, if not stupid, and doesn't behave according to a code. The docile Sleeping Beauty does not have to worry too much about a code. She must lie in a comatose state until a prince rescues her, twice—once from the curse of a fairy and then from the prince's own ogresslike mother. In almost all the tales, Perrault has his female figures suffer, like the martyred Griseldis or the princess in "Donkey-Skin" threatened by her incestuous father, in order to show their strength of character. Their role in Perrault's time was to be one of humble grace. On the other hand, Perrault's male characters are resolute opportunists, similar to many members of his own bourgeois class, who take advantage of situations and do not hesitate to kill to attain power. However, they, too, like the peasant in "Puss in Boots," must respect the code of civility and speak and dress well to attain or maintain the rank of prince. This also holds true for Tom Thumb, the little killer who becomes a royal messenger and rescues his family from poverty.

Perrault's great accomplishments were to produce an immaculate poetic rendition of elegant fairy tales that stemmed from an oral and literary tradition and to transform them into incisive comments about manners and mores at a time when Louis XIV's court was in decline and Louis was destroying France with his wanton wars. His tales read like ironic moral exempla intended to provoke and charm his readers at the same time. He appropriated folklore to refine it and shift many of the meanings to intervene in the social and political debates that pertained to the upper classes. His voice was that of the pseudo Mother Goose, soothing, charming, and assuring, but it was also loaded with Cartesian logic and Jansenite morality intended to provide instruction to young and old alike.

It is indeed ironic that in the course of the eighteenth century after his death—and well throughout the following centuries—Perrault's tales were "reappropriated" by publishers, educators, and common people to become more and more tales for children and for a broad public. Not only were they reprinted in chapbooks or cheap books for lower-class and middle-class households like the Bibliothèque Bleue series in France and in Germany, but they were also widely translated and tailored for children up through the twentieth century to the present.

In recent times, Perrault's tales have been exhaustively examined from different critical perspectives—philological, psychological, feminist, Marxist, historical, anthropological, and so on. Although they have often been "reduced" to children's tales, the scholarly interpretations reveal just how subtle and complex they are and how much they still resonate in "adult" minds. Along with the tales collected by the Brothers Grimm, Perrault's narratives have become the incarnation of canonical literature. That is, they are regarded as the definitive classical fairy tales for children and adults. Yet, this is true primarily in the manner in which they have conserved a basic patriarchal attitude regarding gender roles, social codes of courting, hierarchical familial and political relations, inheritance, and government. Given the "conservative" pallor and high bourgeois refinement of Perrault's tales, it is interesting to consider why Angela Carter would have been attracted to these narratives, much less willing to translate them at the height of the feminist movement in the 1970s.

One could also ask, of course, why Angela Carter used the "perverted" Marquis de Sade about the same time that she was translating Perrault to intervene in the debates about feminism in the 1970s. Carter seemed to have a weakness or perhaps a knack for taking on conservative gentlemen—her father was a staunch conservative Scotsman, proud of Scottish nationalism—and challenging their views and remaking them and their works so that they articulated her views on life and literature. In the case of Perrault, she definitely had to "misinterpret" him and reshape his tales so that they could become more earthy, more in tune with Carter's radical vision of aesthetics and the efficacy of storytelling.

In her afterword to Carter's two Virago collections of international folk tales that focus on female protagonists, Marina Warner has incisively summed up Carter's attitude toward folk and fairy tales: "She was scathing about the contempt the 'educated' can show, when two-thirds of the literature of the world—

perhaps more—has been created by the illiterate. She liked the solid common sense of folk tales, the straightforward aims of their protagonists, the simple moral distinctions, and the wily stratagems they suggest. They are tales of the underdog, about cunning and high spirits winning through in the end, they are practical, and they are not high-flown." If this was indeed Carter's ideological and aesthetic approach to tales and if she was going to translate Perrault's tales, it was impossible for her to accept Perrault as the refined conservative poet that he was and the tales as high literary recondite texts intended to provide examples of civility. He and his tales had to be brought down to earth in her translation—something she did in a much more apparent way in *The Bloody Chamber*—and she did this in her introduction to the tales and in her rewriting of the tales by making him into a gentle educator of children who wrote in a precise, reasonable style and recaptured the folk spirit in "the simplicity of form and the narrative directness of the country story-teller."

Carter's Perrault is Carter's radical reappropriation of Perrault for "children" of the 1970s. As translator, who had to respect Perrault's texts, there were limits to what she could make out of Perrault's tales. But in her own usual sublime way, she tested those limits. In their astute analysis of Carter's translation, Ute Heidmann and Jean-Michel Adam have demonstrated her complex linguistic changes and references that reveal great differences in the "dialogue" Carter maintained with Perrault's texts. Above all there are two tendencies in her translation that are most striking. First, she turned all of the verse morals at the end of each tale into prosaic folksy proverbs that often contradict what Perrault endeavored to communicate. Second, she added numerous phrases to the tales to give them a more "folk" atmosphere consistent with the oral tradition, and she transformed longer sentences into succinct, paratactic phrases reminiscent of simple storytelling. As a result, Carter returns Perrault and his tales to the folk.

Some examples are in order. So let us compare the morals at the end of "Cinderella" and "Sleeping Beauty."

Carter's Moral for "Cinderella"

It is certainly a great advantage to be intelligent, brave, well-born, sensible and have other similar talents given only by heaven. But however great may be your god-given store, they will never help you to get on in the world unless you have either a godfather or a godmother to put them to work for you.

Perrault's Moral for "Cinderella" in a More Literal Translation

Woman's beauty is a treasure
That we never cease to admire,
But a sweet disposition exceeds all measure
And is more dear than a precious gem's fire.
Now the fairy's gift to Cinderella, according to the story,
Was what she taught the girl about love and glory,
And she did it so well that Cinderella became queen.
(Indeed this story has a moral to be esteemed.)

Beautiful ladies, it's kindness more than dress
That can win a man's heart with greater success.
In short, if you want to be blessed,
The real fairy gift is graciousness.

Another Moral

It's undoubtedly a great advantage
To have wit and a good deal of courage,
Or if you're born with common sense
And other worthwhile talents
That heaven may discharge.
But all of these may prove useless
And you may indeed need others
If you think you can have success
Without godfathers or godmothers.[1]

Carter's Moral for "Sleeping Beauty"

A brave, rich, handsome husband is a prize well worth waiting for; but no modern woman would think it was worth waiting for a hundred years. The tale of the Sleeping Beauty shows how long engagements make for happy marriages, but young girls these days want so much to be married I do not have the heart to press the moral.

Perrault's Moral for "Sleeping Beauty" in a More Literal Translation

To wait so long
And want a man rich, refined, sweet and strong
Is not at all uncommon.
And yet it's rare one hundred years
To wait as did this woman
As if she had not woe or care.

Our tale now seems to show
That when marriage is deferred,
There's no less joy than others of which you've heard.
There's nothing lost after a century or so.
And yet there are those lovers whose ardor
Cannot be tamed and they marry out of passion.
Whatever their case I can't deplore,
Or preach a moral lesson.[2]

In both cases, it is clear that Perrault's morals are much more complex, ironic, delicate, and ambivalent than Carter's frank messages to readers, whom she wants to advise in a blunt and succinct manner. Perrault often wrote two morals for a tale, to create contradictions and ambiguity. He purposely played with the proverbs and superstitions of the folk to mock them while also ridiculing the fashions and pretensions of the upper classes. Carter wanted, however, to minimize the elegant Cartesian irony and to transform Perrault into a more traditional storyteller sitting by the fireside. So she begins "Little Red Riding Hood" with "Once upon a time, deep in the heart of the country, there lived a pretty little girl whose mother adored her, and her grandmother adored her even more. This good woman made her a red hood like the ones that fine ladies wear when they go riding. The hood suited the child so much that soon everybody was calling her Little Red Riding Hood." On the other hand, Perrault writes, in a more literal translation: "Once upon a time there was a little village girl, the prettiest that had ever been seen. Her mother doted on her [was crazy about her], and her grandmother even more. This good woman made her a little red cap [chaperon] which suited her so well that she was called Little Red Cap wherever she went."[3] Carter adds phrases to emphasize the country setting and to provide explanations. She does not make drastic changes in the plot or in the characters; she strives for simplicity and sincerity. At the beginning of "Hop o' my Thumb" (often translated as "Little Thumbling" or "Little Tom Thumb"), Carter writes: "A certain woodcutter and his wife were blessed with seven sons. The eldest was ten years old and the youngest seven. It may seem a remarkable feat to produce so many children in so little time but the woodcutter's wife had gone to work with a will and rarely given her husband less than two at once. They were very poor and their seven children were a great inconvenience because none of them could earn their living. The youngest was the greatest inconvenience of all; he was a weakling and a mute, and they mistook his debility for stupidity. He was very, very tiny and when he came into the world he was scarcely bigger than your thumb. So they called him 'Hop o' my Thumb.'"

A more literal translation of Perrault's text reads: "Once upon a time there was a woodcutter and his wife who had seven children, all boys. The eldest was but ten years old, and the youngest only seven. People were astonished that the woodcutter had had so many children in such a short time, but the fact is that his wife did not mince matters and seldom gave birth to less than two at a time. They were very poor, and their seven children were a great burden to them since none of the boys was able to earn his own living. What distressed them even more was that the youngest son was very delicate and never said a word. They mistook his silence for stupidity when it was a mark of great intelligence. Moreover, he was very little. Indeed, at birth he was scarcely bigger than one's thumb so that everyone called him little Tom Thumb."[4]

Carter uses a more contemporary English idiom and cadence and downplays Perrault's ironic attitude toward this poor family. In all his fairy tales, especially in the morals, Perrault exhibits a patronizing attitude with a twinkle in his eye. He wants his readers to know that he does not take the events or characters in his stories very seriously. They are entertaining, as are the lessons that he preaches. Carter has a more jocular sense of humor and sympathizes with many of the persecuted or oppressed protagonists. Hop o' my Thumb is a special case in point. She loved little cunning heroes like this boy, and she cleverly "saves" him from Perrault in her translation, which she ends this way:

> He worked as a special messenger until he saved up a small fortune. Then he went home to his father's house. He took good care of his entire family; he bought peerages for his father and all his brothers and lived in ease and comfort for the rest of his life.
>
> MORAL
>
> It is no affliction to have a large family if they are all handsome, strong and clever. But if one of them is a puny weakling, he will be despised, jeered at and mocked. However, often the runt of the litter ends up making the family fortune.

A more literal translation reads:

> After he had been a courier for some time and saved a good deal of money, he returned to his father, and you cannot imagine how joyful his family was at seeing him again. He made them all comfortable by buying newly created titled positions for his father and brothers. In this way he made sure they were all established, and at the same time, he made certain that he did perfectly well at the court himself.

Moral

No longer are children said to be a hardship,
If they possess great charm, good looks, and wit.
If one is weak, however, and knows not what to say,
Mocked he'll be and chased until he runs far away.
Yet, sometimes it's this child, very least expected,
Who makes his fortune and has his honor resurrected.[5]

Carter could not let "the runt of the litter"—what a wonderful translation!—spend his final days at court as some kind of opportunist who has finally arrived and made a place for himself in high society. Hop o' my Thumb is a family man, a provider, and Carter's version of Perrault's tale is told in a clipped, gritty style that recalls tales told at the hearth.

Translating is not a mechanical art. Every time a work is translated it is re-created in many different ways, not only to communicate the "original" meaning of an author's work, but also to communicate the translator's personal view of what an author may have meant and what she thinks will make that particular author's work most accessible and meaningful in a different period of time and in another culture. Perrault inspired Carter to delve more deeply into the origins and meanings of fairy tales, but she had to misread him or reinterpret him to make his tales more palatable to her feminist and political sensitivity. Clearly she sensed the problematic aspects of Perrault's style and ideology, which she purposely glossed over in her translation, and this may have made her so dissatisfied that she was "driven" to revisit Perrault's tales in a dramatically and radically different way in *The Bloody Chamber,* while she was translating Perrault's tales. What is fascinating about the tales in *The Bloody Chamber,* most of them based on Perrault's stories, is that they are written in a contemporary baroque sensuous and luscious language with extraordinary metaphors that recall the seventeenth-century fairy tales of Giambattista Basile, who combined Neapolitan vulgar dialect with the mannerist and affected language of the upper classes. Basile relished mocking both the upper classes and the peasantry. Perrault was not much different, but he tended to soothe the sensibilities and to appease his upper-class readers. Carter rarely appeased anyone. Her remake of Perrault's tales is her intrepid endeavor to transform Perrault's refined stories and return them to the folk of all ages. They bristle with dynamic common sense and a joyful optimism that would charm the pants off the meanest of raucous readers.

—JACK ZIPES

NOTES

1. La beauté pour le sexe est un rare trésor,
De l'admirer jamais on ne se lasse;
Mais ce qu'on nomme bonne grâce
Est sans prix, et vaut mieux encor.
C'est ce qu'à Cendrillon fit avoir sa Marraine
En la dressant, en l'instruisant,
Tant et si bien qu'elle en fit une Reine:
(Car ainsi sur ce Conte on va moralisant.)

Belles, ce don vaut mieux que d'être bien coiffées,
Pour engager un cœur, pour en venir à bout,
La bonne grâce est le vrai don des Fées;
Sans elle on ne peut rien, avec elle, on peut tout.

AUTRE MORALITÉ

C'est sans doute un grand avantage,
D'avoir de l'esprit, du courage,
De la naissance, du bon sens,
Et d'autres semblables talents,
Qu'on reçoit du Ciel en partage;
Pour votre avancement ce seront choses vaines,
Si vous n'avez, pour les faire valoir,
Ou des parrains ou des marraines.

2. Attendre quelque temps pour avoir un Époux,
Riche, bien fait, galant et doux,
La chose est assez naturelle,
Mais l'attendre cents ans, et toujours en dormant,
On ne trouve pas plus de femelle,
Qui dormît si tranquillement.

La Fable semble encor vouloir nous faire entrendre
Que souvent de l'Hymen les agréables nœuds,
Pour être differes, n'en sont pas moins heureux,
Et qu'on ne perd rien pour attendre;
Mais le sexe avec tant d'ardeur,
Aspire à la foi conjugale,
Que je n'ai pas la force ni le cœur,
De lui prêcher cette morale.

3. Il était une fois une petite fille de Village, la plus jolie qu'on eût su voir; sa mère en était folle, et sa mère-grand plus folle encore. Cette bonne femme lui fit faire un petit chaperon rouge, qui lui seyait si bien, que partout on l'appelait le Petit Chaperon rouge.

4. Il était une fois un Bûcheron et une Bûcherone qui avaient sept enfants. L'aîné n'avait que dix ans, et le plus jeune n'en avait que sept. On s'étonnera que le Bûcheron ait eut tant d'enfants en si peu de temps; mais c'est que sa femme allait vite en besogne, et n'en faisait pas moins que deux à la fois. Ils étaient fort pauvres, et leurs sept enfants les incommodaient beaucoup, parce qu'aucun d'eux ne pouvait encore gagner sa vie. Ce qui les chagrinait encore, c'est que le plus jeune était for délicat et ne disait mot; prenant pour bêtise ce qui était une marque de la bonté de son esprit. Il était fort petit, et quand il vint au monde, il n'était guère plus gros que le puce, ce qui fit qu'on l'appela le petit Poucet.

5. Après avoir fait pendant quelque temps le métier de courrier, et y avoir amassé beaucoup de bien, il revint chez son père, où il n'est pas possible d'imaginer la joie qu'on eut de le revoir. Il mit toute sa famille à son aise. Il acheta des Offices de nouvelle création pour son père et pour ses frères; et par là il les établit tous, et fit parfaitement bien sa Cour en même temps.

MORALITÉ

On ne s'afflige point d'avoir beaucoup d'enfants,
Quand ils sont tous beaux, bien faits et bien grands,
Et d'un extérieur qui brille;
Mais si l'un d'eux est faible ou ne dit mot,
On le méprise, on le raille, on le pille;
Quelquefois cependant c'est ce petit marmot
Qui fera le bonheur de toute la famille.

Suggestions for Further Reading

ANGELA CARTER

Atwood, Margaret. "Running with the Tigers," *Flesh and Mirror: Essays on the Art of Angela Carter.* Ed. Lorna Sage. London: Virago, 1994. 117–35.

———. "Angela Carter: 1940–1992," *Curious Pursuits: Occasional Writing,* 1970–2005. London: Virago, 2005. 155–57.

Barchilon, Jacques. "Remembering Angela Carter," *Marvels & Tales* 12.1 (1998): 19–22.

Benson, Stephen. "Angela Carter and the Literary *Märchen:* A Review Essay." *Marvels & Tales* 12.1 (1998): 23–51.

Day, Aidan. *Angela Carter: The Rational Glass.* Manchester: University of Manchester Press, 1994.

Easton, Alison, ed. *Angela Carter.* New York: St. Martin's Press, 2000.

Gamble, Sarah. *The Fiction of Angela Carter.* London: Palgrave, 2003.

———. *Angela Carter: A Literary Life.* New York: Palgrave, 2006.

Lee, Alison. *Angela Carter.* New York: Twayne, 1997.

Munford, Rebecca, ed. *Re-visiting Angela Carter.* New York: Palgrave, 2006.

Roemer, Danielle, and Cristina Bacchilega, eds. *Angela Carter and the Fairy Tale.* Detroit: Wayne State University Press, 2001.

Rushdie, Salman. "Angela Carter, 1940–92: A Very Good Wizard, a Very Dear Friend," *New York Times Book Review* (March 8, 1992): 5.

Sage, Lorna, ed. *Flesh and the Mirror: Essays on the Art of Angela Carter*. London: Virago, 1994.

———. "Angela Carter and the Fairy Tale." *Marvels & Tales* 12.1 (1998): 52–68.

Warner, Marina. "Afterword." In *Angela Carter's Book of Fairy Tales*. Ed. Angela Carter. London: Virago, 2005. 447–54.

Zipes, Jack. "Crossing Boundaries with Wise Girls: Angela Carter's Fairy Tales for Children," *Marvels & Tales* 12.1 (1998): 159–66.

SELECTED FAIRY-TALE WORKS BY ANGELA CARTER

The Donkey Prince. Illus. Eros Keith. New York: Simon & Schuster, 1970.

Miss Z. the Dark Lady. Illus. Eros Keith. New York: Simon & Schuster, 1970.

The Fairy Tales of Charles Perrault. Illus. Martin Ware. London: Gollancz, 1977.

The Bloody Chamber and Other Stories. London: Penguin, 1979.

Ed. *Sleeping Beauty and other Favourite Fairy Tales*. Illus. Michael Foreman. London: Gollancz, 1982.

Ed. *The Virago Book of Fairy Tales*. Illus. Corinna Sargood. London: Virago, 1990. Rpt. as *The Old Wives Fairy Tale Book*. New York: Pantheon, 1990.

Ed. *The Second Virago Book of Fairy Tales*. Illus. Corinna Sargood. London: Virago, 1992. Rpt. As *Strange Things Still Happen: Fairy Tales from Around the World*. Boston and London: Faber and Faber, 1993.

CHARLES PERRAULT

Barchilon, Jacques, and Peter Flinders. *Charles Perrault*. Boston: Twayne, 1981.

Burne, Glenn S., "Charles Perrault 1628–1703," in *Writers for Children: Critical Studies of Major Authors Since the Seventeenth Century.* Ed. Jane M. Bingham. New York: Scribners, 1988.

Hannon, Patricia. *Fabulous Identities: Women's Fairy Tales in Seventeenth-Century France.* Amsterdam: Rodopi, 1998.

Harries, Elizabeth W. "Simulating Oralities: French Fairy Tales of the 1690s." *College Literature* 23 (June 1996): 100–15.

Heidmann, Ute, and Jean Michel Adam. "Text Linguistics and Comparative Literature: Towards an Interdisciplinary Approach to Written Tales. Angela Carter's Translations of Perrault," in *Language and Verbal Art Revisited: Linguistic Approaches to the Literature Text.* Ed. Donna R. Millere and Monica Turci. London: Equinox, 2007. 181–96.

Lewis, Philip. *Seeing through the Mother Goose Tales: Visual Turns in the Writings of Charles Perrault.* Stanford: Stanford University Press, 1996.

Marin, Louis. "La cuisine des fées: or the Culinary Sign in the Tales of Perrault." *Genre,* 16.4 (1983): 477–83.

Morgan, Jeanne. *Perrault's Morals for Moderns.* New York: Peter Lang, 1985.

McGlathery, James M. *Fairy Tale Romance: the Grimms, Basile, and Perrault.* Urbana: University of Illinois Press, 1991.

Seifert, Lewis C. "Disguising the Storyteller's 'Voice': Perrault's Recuperation of the Fairy Tale." *Cincinnati Romance Review* 8 (1989), 18–23.

———. *Fairy Tales, Sexuality, and Gender in France, 1690–1715: Nostalgic Utopias.* Cambridge: University of Cambridge Press, 1996.

Soriano, Marc. *Les Contes de Perrault. Culture savante et traditions populaires.* Paris: Gallimard, 1968.

Velay-Vallantin, Catherine. *Special Issue of Marvels & Tales on Charles Perrault.* 5.2 (December 1991). This issue contains essays on Perrault's tales by Catherine Velay-Vallantin, Jacques Barchilon, Marie-Dominique Leclerc, Claire Malarte-Feldman, Jacques Berlioz, Mariette Larvor, Paola Pallottino, Hans-Jög Uther, Harold Neemann, and Jean-Louis Hippolyte.

Warner, Marina. *From the Beast to the Blonde: On Fairy Tales and their Tellers*. London: Chatto & Windus, 1995.
Zipes, Jack. *Fairy Tales and the Art of Subversion: The Classical Genre for Children and the Process of Civilization*. 2nd Rev. and Expanded Ed. New York: Routledge, 2006.

SELECTED MODERN FRENCH EDITIONS OF PERRAULT'S FAIRY TALES

Contes de Perrault. Ed. Gilbert Rouger. Paris: Garnier, 1967.
Contes de Perrault. Ed. Jean Pierre Collinet. Folio, 1281. Paris: Gallimard, 1981.
Contes de Perrault. Ed. Marc Soriano. Paris: Flammarion, 1989.
Contes de Perrault. Ed. Catherine Magnien. Paris: Le Livre de Poche, 1990.

All of these editions have excellent introductions with copious notes.

The Fairy Tales of Charles Perrault

Little Red Riding Hood

Once upon a time, deep in the heart of the country, there lived a pretty little girl whose mother adored her, and her grandmother adored her even more. This good woman made her a red hood like the ones that fine ladies wear when they go riding. The hood suited the child so much that soon everybody was calling her Little Red Riding Hood.

One day, her mother baked some cakes on the griddle and said to Little Red Riding Hood:

"Your granny is sick; you must go and visit her. Take her one of these cakes and a little pot of butter."

Little Red Riding Hood went off to the next village to visit her grandmother. As she walked through the wood, she met a wolf, who wanted to eat her but did not dare to because there were woodcutters working nearby. He asked her where she was going. The poor child did not know how dangerous it is to chatter away to wolves and replied innocently:

"I'm going to visit my grandmother to take her this cake and this little pot of butter from my mother."

"Does your grandmother live far away?" asked the wolf.

"Oh, yes," said Little Red Riding Hood. "She lives beyond the mill you can see over there, in the first house you come to in the village."

"Well, I shall go and visit her, too," said the wolf. "I will take *this* road and you shall take *that* road and let's see who can get there first."

The wolf ran off by the shortest path and Red Riding Hood went off the longest way and she made it still longer because she dawdled along, gathering nuts and chasing butterflies and picking bunches of wayside flowers.

The wolf soon arrived at Grandmother's house. He knocked on the door, rat tat tat.

"Who's there?"

"Your grand-daughter, Little Red Riding Hood," said the wolf, disguisng his voice. "I've brought you a cake baked on the griddle and a little pot of butter from my mother."

Grandmother was lying in bed because she was poorly. She called out:

"Lift up the latch and walk in!"

The wolf lifted the latch and opened the door. He had not eaten for three days. He threw himself on the good woman and gobbled her up. Then he closed the door behind him and lay down in Grandmother's bed to wait for Little Red Riding Hood. At last she came knocking on the door, rat tat tat.

"Who's there?"

Little Red Riding Hood heard the hoarse voice of the wolf and thought that her grandmother must have caught a cold. She answered:

"It's your grand-daughter, Little Red Riding Hood. I've brought you a cake baked on the griddle and a little pot of butter from my mother."

The wolf disguised his voice and said:

"Lift up the latch and walk in."

Little Red Riding Hood lifted the latch and opened the door. When the wolf saw her come in, he hid himself under the bedclothes and said to her:

"Put the cake and the butter down on the bread-bin and come and lie down with me."

Little Red Riding Hood took off her clothes and went to lie down in the bed. She was surprised to see how odd her grandmother looked. She said to her:

"Grandmother, what big arms you have!"

"All the better to hold you with, my dear."

"Grandmother, what big legs you have!"

"All the better to run with, my dear."

"Grandmother, what big ears you have!"

"All the better to hear with, my dear."

"Grandmother, what big eyes you have!"

"All the better to see with, my dear!"

"Grandmother, what big teeth you have!"

"All the better to eat you up!"

At that, the wicked wolf threw himself upon Little Red Riding Hood and gobbled her up, too.

MORAL

Children, especially pretty, nicely brought-up young ladies, ought never to talk to strangers; if they are foolish enough to do so, they should not be surprised if some greedy wolf consumes them, elegant red riding hoods and all.

Now, there are real wolves, with hairy pelts and enormous teeth; but also wolves who seem perfectly charming, sweet-natured and obliging, who pursue young girls in the street and pay them the most flattering attentions.

Unfortunately, these smooth-tongued, smooth-pelted wolves are the most dangerous beasts of all.

Bluebeard

There once lived a man who owned fine town houses and fine country houses, dinner services of gold and silver, tapestry chairs and gilded coaches; but, alas, God had also given him a blue beard, which made him look so ghastly that women fled at the sight of him.

A certain neighbour of his was the mother of two beautiful daughters. He decided to marry one or other of them, but he left the girls to decide between themselves which of them should become his wife; whoever would take him could have him. But neither of them wanted him; both felt a profound distaste for a man with a blue beard. They were even more suspicious of him because he had been married several times before and nobody knew what had become of his wives.

In order to make friends with the girls, Bluebeard threw a lavish house-party at one of his country mansions for the sisters, their mother, three or four of their closest friends and several neighbours. The party lasted for eight whole days. Every day there were elaborate parties of pleasure—fishing, hunting, dancing, games, feasting. The guests hardly slept at all but spent the night playing practical jokes on one another. Everything went so well that the youngest daughter began to think that the beard of the master of the house was not so very blue, after all; that he was, all in all, a very fine fellow.

As soon as they returned to town, the marriage took place.

After a month had passed, Bluebeard told his wife he must leave her to her own devices for six weeks or so; he had urgent business in the provinces and must attend to it immediately.

But he urged her to enjoy herself while he was away; her friends should visit her and, if she wished, she could take them to the country with her. But, above all, she must keep in good spirits.

"Look!" he said to her. "Here are the keys of my two large attics, where the furniture is stored; this is the key to the cabinet in which I keep the dinner services of gold and silver that are too good to use every day; these are the keys of the strong-boxes in which I keep my money; these are the keys of my chests of precious stones; and this is the pass key that will let you into every one of the rooms in my mansion. Use these keys freely. All is yours. But this little key, here, is the key of the room at the end of the long gallery on the ground floor; open everything, go everywhere, but I absolutely forbid you to go into that little room and, if you so much as open the door, I warn you that nothing will spare you from my wrath."

She promised to do as he told her. He kissed her, got into his carriage and drove away.

Her friends and neighbours did not wait until she sent for them to visit her. They were all eager to see the splendours of her house. None of them had dared to call while the master was at home because his blue beard was so offensive. But now they could explore all the rooms at leisure and each one was more sumptuous than the last. They climbed into the attics and were lost for words with which to admire the number and beauty of the tapestries, the beds, the sofas, the cabinets, the tables, and the long mirrors, some of which had frames of glass, others of silver or gilded vermilion—all more magnificent than anything they had ever seen. They never stopped congratulating their friend on her good luck, but she took no pleasure from the sight of all this luxury because she was utterly consumed with the desire to open the door of the forbidden room.

Her curiosity so tormented her that, at last, without stopping to think how rude it was to leave her friends, she ran down the little staircase so fast she almost tripped and broke her neck. When she reached the door of the forbidden room, she stopped for a moment and remembered that her husband had absolutely forbidden her to go inside. She wondered if he would punish her for being disobedient; but the temptation was so strong she could not resist it. She took the little key, and, trembling, opened the door.

The windows were shuttered and at first she could see nothing; but, after a few moments, her eyes grew accustomed to the gloom and she saw that the floor was covered with clotted blood. In the blood lay the corpses of all the women whom Bluebeard had married and then murdered, one after the other. She thought she was going to die of fright and the key fell from her hand. After she came to her senses, she picked up the key, closed the door and climbed back to her room to recover herself.

She saw the key of this forbidden room was stained with blood and washed it. But the blood would not go away, so she washed it again. Still the blood-stain stayed. She washed it, yet again, more carefully, then scrubbed it with soap and sandstone; but the blood-stain would not budge. It was a magic key and nothing could clean it. When the blood was scrubbed from one side of the key, the stain immediately reappeared on the other side.

That same night, Bluebeard returned unexpectedly from his journey; a letter had arrived on the way to tell him that his business had already been satisfactorily settled in his absence. His wife did all she could to show him how delighted she was to have him back with her so quickly.

Next day, he asked for his keys; she gave them to him but her hand was trembling so badly he guessed what had happened.

"How is it that the key of the little room is no longer with the others?" he asked.

"I must have left it upstairs on my dressing-table," she said, flustered.

"Give it to me," said Bluebeard.

She made excuse after excuse but there was no way out; she must go and fetch the key. Bluebeard examined it carefully and said to his wife:

"Why is there blood on this key?"

"I don't know," quavered the poor woman, paler than death.

"You don't know!" said Bluebeard. "But *I* know, very well! You have opened the door of the forbidden room. Well, madame, now you have opened it, you may step straight inside it and take your place beside the ladies whom you have seen there!"

She threw herself at her husband's feet, weeping and begging his forgiveness; she was truly sorry she had been disobedient. She was so beautiful and so distressed that the sight of her would have melted a heart of stone, but Bluebeard's heart was harder than any stone.

"You must die, madame," he said. "And you must die quickly."

She looked at him with eyes full of tears and pleaded:

"Since I must die, give me a little time to pray."

Bluebeard said: "I'll give you a quarter of an hour, but not one moment more."

As soon as she was alone, she called to her sister, Anne, and said:

"Sister Anne, climb to the top of the tower and see if my brothers are coming; they told me they would come to visit me today and if you see them, signal to them to hurry."

Sister Anne climbed to the top of the tower and the poor girl called out to her every minute or so:

"Sister Anne, Sister Anne, do you see anybody coming?"

And Anne, her sister, would reply:

"I see nothing but the sun shining and the grass growing green."

Bluebeard took an enormous cutlass in his hand and shouted to his wife: "Come down at once, or I'll climb up to you!"

"Oh, please, I beg you—just a moment more!" she implored, and called out, in a lower voice: "Sister Anne, Sister Anne, do you see anybody coming?"

Sister Anne replied:

"I see nothing but the sun shining and the grass growing green."

"Come down at once, or I'll climb up to you!" cried Bluebeard.

"I'll be down directly," his wife assured him; but still she whispered: "Sister Anne, Sister Anne, do you see anything coming?"

"I see a great cloud of dust drawing near from the edge of the horizon."

"Is it the dust my brothers make as they ride towards me?"

"Oh, no—it is the dust raised by a flock of sheep!"

"Will you never come down?" thundered Bluebeard.

"Just one moment more!" begged his wife and once again she demanded: "Sister Anne, Sister Anne, do you see anything coming?"

"I see two horsemen in the distance, still far away. Thank God!" she cried a moment later. "They are our brothers; I shall signal to them to hurry."

Bluebeard now shouted so loudly that all the house trembled. His unfortunate wife went down to him and threw herself in tears at his feet, her dishevelled hair tumbling around her.

"Nothing you can do will save you," said Bluebeard. "You must die." With one hand, he seized her disordered hair and, with the other, raised his cutlass in the air; he meant to chop off her head with it. The poor woman turned her terrified eyes upon him and begged him for a last moment in which to prepare for death.

"No, no!" he said. "Think of your maker." And so he lifted up his cutlass. At that moment came such a loud banging on the door that Bluebeard stopped short. The door opened and in rushed two horsemen with naked blades in their hands.

He recognised his wife's two brothers; one was a dragoon, the other a musketeer. He fled, to save himself, but the two brothers trapped him before he reached the staircase. They thrust their swords through him and left him for dead. Bluebeard's wife was almost as overcome as her husband and did not have enough strength left to get to her feet and kiss her brothers.

Bluebeard left no heirs, so his wife took possession of all his estate. She used part of it to marry her sister Anne to a young man with whom she had been in love for a long time; she used more of it to buy commissions for her two brothers; and she used the rest to marry herself to an honest man who made her forget her sorrows as the wife of Bluebeard.

MORAL

Curiosity is a charming passion but may only be satisfied at the price of a thousand regrets; one sees around one a thousand examples of this sad truth every day. Curiosity is the most fleeting of pleasures; the moment it is satisfied, it ceases to exist and it always proves very, very expensive.

ANOTHER MORAL

It is easy to see that the events described in this story took place many years ago. No modern husband would dare to be half so terrible, nor to demand of his wife such an impossible thing as to stifle her curiosity. Be he never so quarrelsome or jealous, he'll toe the line as soon as she tells him to. And whatever colour his beard might be, it's easy to see which of the two is the master.

Puss in Boots

A certain poor miller had only his mill, his ass and his cat to bequeath to his three sons when he died. The children shared out their patrimony and did not bother to call in the lawyers; if they had done so, they would have been stripped quite bare, of course. The eldest took the mill, the second the ass and the youngest had to make do with the cat.

He felt himself very ill used.

"My brothers can earn an honest living with their inheritance, but once I've eaten my cat and made a muff with his pelt, I shall have to die of hunger."

The cat overheard him but decided to pretend he had not done so; he addressed his master gravely.

"Master, don't fret; give me a bag and a pair of boots to protect my little feet from the thorny undergrowth and you'll see that your father hasn't provided for you so badly, after all."

Although the cat's master could not really believe his cat would support him, he had seen him play so many cunning tricks when he went to catch rats and mice—he would hang upside down by his feet; or hide himself in the meal and play at being dead—that he felt a faint hope his cat might think up some helpful scheme.

When the cat had got what he asked for, he put on his handsome boots and slung the bag round his neck, keeping hold of the draw-strings with his two front paws. He went to a warren where he knew there were a great many rabbits. He put some bran and a selection of juicy weeds at the bottom of the bag and then stretched out quite still, like a corpse, and waited for some ingenuous young rabbit to come and investigate the bag and its appetising contents.

No sooner had he lain down than a silly bunny jumped into the bag. Instantly, the cat pulled the draw-strings tight and killed the rabbit without mercy.

Proudly bearing his prey, he went to the king and asked to speak to him. He was taken to his majesty's private apartment. As soon as he got inside the door, he made the king a tremendous bow and said:

"Sire, may I present you with a delicious young rabbit that my master, the Marquis of Carabas, ordered me to offer to you, with his humblest compliments."

Without his master's knowledge or consent, the cat had decided the miller's son should adopt the name of the Marquis of Carabas.

"Tell your master that I thank him with all my heart," said the king.

The next day, the cat hid himself in a cornfield, with his open bag, and two partridges flew into it. He pulled the strings and caught them both. Then he went to present them to the king, just as he had done with the rabbit. The king accepted the partridges with great glee and rewarded the cat with a handsome tip.

The cat kept on taking his master's game to the king for two or three months. One day, he learned that the king planned to take a drive along the riverside with his beautiful daughter. He said to his master:

"If you take my advice, your fortune is made. You just go for a swim in the river at a spot I'll show to you and leave the rest to me."

The Marquis of Carabas obediently went off to swim, although he could not think why the cat should want him to. While he was bathing, the king drove by and the cat cried out with all its might:

"Help! Help! The Marquis of Carabas is drowning!"

The king put his head out of his carriage window when he heard this commotion and recognised the cat who had brought him so much game. He ordered his servants to hurry and save the Marquis of Carabas.

While they were pulling the marquis out of the river, the cat went to the king's carriage and told him how robbers had stolen his master's clothes while he swam in the river even though he'd shouted "Stop thief!" at the top of his voice. In fact, the cunning cat had hidden the miller's son's wretched clothes under a stone.

The king ordered the master of his wardrobe to hurry back to the palace and bring a selection of his own finest garments for the Marquis of Carabas to wear. When the young man put them on, he looked very handsome and the king's daughter thought: "What an attractive young man!" The Marquis of Carabas treated her with respect mingled with tenderness and she fell madly in love.

The king invited the Marquis of Carabas to join him in his carriage and continue the drive in style. The cat was delighted to see his scheme begin to succeed and busily ran ahead of the procession. He came to a band of peasants who were mowing a meadow and said:

"Good people, if you don't tell the king that this meadow belongs to the Marquis of Carabas, I'll make mincemeat of every one of you."

As soon as he saw the mowers, the king asked them who owned the hayfield. They had been so intimidated by the cat that they dutifully chorused:

"It belongs to the Marquis of Carabas."

"You have a fine estate," remarked the king to the marquis.

"The field crops abundantly every year," improvised the marquis.

The cat was still racing ahead of the party and came to a band of harvesters. He said to them:

"Good harvesters, if you don't say that all these cornfields belong to the Marquis of Carabas, I'll make mincemeat of every one of you."

The king passed by a little later and wanted to know who owned the rolling cornfield.

"The Marquis of Carabas possesses them all," said the harvesters.

The king expressed his increasing admiration of the marquis' estates. The cat ran before the carriage and made the same threats to everyone he met on the way; the king was perfectly astonished at the young man's great possessions.

At last the cat arrived at a castle. In this castle, lived an ogre. This ogre was extraordinarily rich; he was the true owner of all the land through which the king had travelled. The cat had taken good care to find out all he could about this ogre and now he asked the servant who answered the door if he could speak to him; he said he couldn't pass so close by the castle without paying his respects to such an important man as its owner.

The ogre made him as welcome as an ogre can.

"I'm told you can transform yourself into all sorts of animals," said the cat. "That you can change yourself into a lion, for example; or even an elephant."

"Quite right," replied the ogre. "Just to show you, I'll turn myself into a lion."

When he found himself face to face with a lion, even our cat was so scared that he jumped up on to the roof and balanced there precariously because his boots weren't made for walking on tiles.

As soon as the ogre had become himself again, the cat clambered down and confessed how terrified he had been.

"But gossip also has it—though I can scarcely believe it—that you also have the power to take the shapes of the very smallest animals. They say you can even shrink down as small as a rat, or a mouse. But I must admit, even if it seems rude, that I think that's quite impossible."

"Impossible?" said the ogre. "Just you see!" He changed into a mouse and began to scamper around on the floor. The cat no sooner saw him than he jumped on him and gobbled him up.

Meanwhile, the king saw the ogre's fine castle as he drove by and decided to pay it a visit. The cat heard the sound of carriage wheels on the drawbridge, ran outside and greeted the king.

"Welcome, your majesty, to the castle of the Marquis of Carabas."

"What, sir? Does this fine castle also belong to you? I've never seen anything more splendid than this courtyard and the battlements that surround it; may we be permitted to view the interior?"

The marquis gave his hand to the young princess and followed the king. They entered a grand room where they found a banquet ready prepared; the ogre had invited all his friends to a dinner party, but none of the guests dared enter the castle when they saw the king had arrived. The king was delighted with the good qualities of the Marquis of Carabas and his daughter was beside herself about them. There was also the young man's immense wealth to be taken into account. After his fifth or sixth glass of wine, the king said:

"Say the word, my fine fellow, and you shall become my son-in-law."

The marquis bowed very low, immediately accepted the honour the king bestowed on him and married the princess that very day. The cat was made a great lord and gave up hunting mice, except for pleasure.

MORAL

A great inheritance may be a fine thing; but hard work and ingenuity will take a young man further than his father's money.

ANOTHER MORAL

If a miller's son can so quickly win the heart of a princess, that is because clothes, bearing and youth speedily inspire affection; and the means to achieve them are not always entirely commendable.

The Sleeping Beauty in the Wood

Once upon a time, there lived a king and a queen who were bitterly unhappy because they did not have any children. They visited all the clinics, all the specialists, made holy vows, went on pilgrimages and said their prayers regularly but with so little success that when, at long last, the queen finally *did* conceive and, in due course, gave birth to a daughter, they were both wild with joy. Obviously, this baby's christening must be the grandest of all possible christenings; for her godmothers, she would have as many fairies as they could find in the entire kingdom. According to the custom of those times, each fairy would make the child a magic present, so that the princess could acquire every possible perfection. After a long search, they managed to trace seven suitable fairies.

After the ceremony at the church, the guests went back to the royal palace for a party in honour of the fairy godmothers. Each of these important guests found her place was specially laid with a great dish of gold and a golden knife, fork and spoon studded with diamonds and rubies. But as the fairies took their seats, an uninvited guest came storming into the palace, deeply affronted because she had been forgotten—though it was no wonder she'd been overlooked; this old fairy had hidden herself away in her tower for fifteen years and, since nobody had set eyes on her all that time, they thought she was dead, or had been bewitched. The king ordered a place to be laid for her at once but he could not give her a great gold dish and gold cutlery like the other fairies had because only seven sets had been made. The old fairy was very annoyed at that and muttered threats between her teeth. The fairy who sat beside her overheard her and suspected she planned to revenge herself by giving the little princess a very unpleasant present when the time for present giving came. She slipped away behind the tapestry so that she could have the last word, if necessary, and put right any harm the old witch might do the baby.

Now the fairies presented their gifts. The youngest fairy said the princess would grow up to be the loveliest woman in the world. The next said she would have the disposition of an angel, the third that she would be graceful as a gazelle, the fourth gave her the gift of dancing, the fifth of singing like a nightingale, and the sixth said she would be able to play any kind of musical instrument that she wanted to.

But when it came to the old fairy's turn, she shook with spite and announced that, in spite of her beauty and accomplishments, the princess was going to prick her finger with a spindle and die of it.

All the guests trembled and wept. But the youngest fairy stepped out from behind the tapestry and cried out:

"Don't despair, King and Queen; your daughter will not die—though, alas, I cannot undo entirely the magic of a senior-ranking fairy. The princess *will* prick her finger with a spindle but, instead of dying, she will fall into a deep sleep that will last for a hundred years. And at the end of a hundred years, the son of a king will come to wake her."

In spite of this comfort, the king did all he could to escape the curse; he forbade the use of a spindle, or even the possession of one, on pain of death, in all the lands he governed.

Fifteen or sixteen years went by. The king and queen were spending the summer at a castle in the country and one day the princess decided to explore, prowling through room after room until at last she climbed up a spiral staircase in a tower and came to an attic in which an old lady was sitting, along with her distaff, spinning, for this old lady had not heard how the king had banned the use of a spindle.

"Whatever are you doing, my good woman?" asked the princess.

"I'm spinning, my pretty dear," answered the old lady.

"Oh, how clever!" said the princess. "How do you do it? Give it to me so that I can see if I can do it, too!"

She was very lively and just a little careless; but besides, and most importantly, the fairies had ordained it. No sooner had she picked up the spindle than she pierced her hand with it and fell down in a faint.

The old lady cried for help and the servants came running from all directions. They threw water over her, unlaced her corsets, slapped her hands, rubbed her temples with eau-de-cologne—but nothing would wake her.

The king climbed to the attic to see the cause of the clamour and, sad at heart, knew the fairy's curse had come true. He knew the princess' time had come, just as the fairies said it would, and ordered her to be carried to the finest room in the palace and laid there on a bed covered with gold and silver embroidery. She was as beautiful as an angel. Her trance had not yet taken the colour from her face; her cheeks were rosy and her lips like coral. Her eyes were closed but you could hear her breathing very, very softly and, if you saw the slow movement of her breast, you knew she was not dead.

The king ordered she should be left in peace until the time came when she would wake up. At the moment the princess had pricked her finger, the good fairy who saved her life was in the realm of Mataquin, twelve thousand leagues away, but she heard the news immediately from a dwarf who sped to her in a pair of seven-league boots. The fairy left Mataquin at once in a fiery chariot drawn by dragons and arrived at the grieving court an hour later. The king went out to help her down; she approved of all his arrangements but she was very sensitive, and she thought how sad the princess would be when she woke up all alone in that great castle.

So she touched everything in the house, except for the king and queen, with her magic ring—the housekeepers, the maids of honour, the chambermaids, the gentlemen-in-waiting, the court officials, the cooks, the scullions, the errand-boys, the night-watchmen, the Swiss guards, the page-boys, the footmen; she touched all the horses in the stable, and the stable-boys, too, and even Puff, the princess' little lap-dog, who was curled up on her bed beside her. As soon as she touched them with her magic ring, they all fell fast asleep and would not wake up until their mistress woke, ready to look after her when she needed them. Even the spits on the fire, loaded with partridges and pheasants, drowsed off to sleep, and the flames died down and slept, too. All this took only a moment; fairies are fast workers.

The king and queen kissed their darling child but she did not stir. Then they left the palace forever and issued proclamations forbidding anyone to approach it. Within a quarter of an hour, a great number of trees, some large, some small, interlaced with brambles and thorns, sprang up around the park and formed a hedge so thick that neither man nor beast could penetrate it. This hedge grew so tall that you could see only the topmost turrets of the castle, for the fairy had made a safe, magic place where the princess could sleep her sleep out free from prying eyes.

At the end of a hundred years, the son of the king who now ruled over the country went out hunting in that region. He asked the local police what those turrets he could see above the great wood might mean. They replied, each one, as he had heard tell—how it was an old ruin, full of ghosts; or, that all the witches of the country went there to hold their sabbaths. But the most popular story was, that it was the home of an ogre who carried all the children he caught there, to eat them at his leisure, knowing nobody else could follow him through the wood.

The prince did not know what to believe. Then an old man said to him:

"My lord, fifty years ago I heard my father say that the most beautiful princess in all the world was sleeping in that castle, and her sleep was going to last for a hundred years, until the prince who is meant to have her comes to wake her up."

When he heard that, the young prince was tremendously excited; he had never heard of such a marvellous adventure and, fired with thoughts of love and glory, he made up his mind there and then to go through the wood. No sooner had he stepped among the trees than the great trunks and branches, the thorns and brambles parted, to let him pass. He saw the castle at the end of a great avenue and walked towards it, though he was surprised to see that none of his attendants could follow him because the trees sprang together again as soon as he had gone between them. But he did not abandon his quest. A young prince in love is always brave. Then he arrived at a courtyard that seemed like a place where only fear lived.

An awful silence filled it and the look of death was on everything. Man and beast stretched on the ground, like corpses; but the pimples on the red noses of the Swiss guards soon showed him they were not dead at all, but sleeping, and the glasses beside them, with the dregs of wine still at the bottoms, showed how they had dozed off after a spree.

He went through a marble courtyard; he climbed a staircase; he went into a guardroom, where the guards were lined up in two ranks, each with a gun on his shoulder, and snoring with all their might. He found several rooms full of gentlemen-in-waiting and fine ladies; some stood, some sat, all slept. At last he arrived in a room that was entirely covered in gilding and, there on a bed with the curtains drawn back so that he could see her clearly, lay a princess about fifteen or sixteen years old and she was so lovely that she seemed, almost, to shine. The prince approached her trembling, and fell on his knees before her.

The enchantment was over; the princess woke. She gazed at him so tenderly you would not have thought it was the first time she had ever seen him.

"Is it you, my prince?" she said. "You have kept me waiting for a long time."

The prince was beside himself with joy when he heard that and the tenderness in her voice overwhelmed him so that he hardly knew how to reply. He told her he loved her better than he loved himself and though he stumbled over the words, that made her very happy, because he showed so much feeling. He was more tongue-tied than she, because she had had plenty of time to dream of what she would say to him; her good fairy had made sure she had sweet dreams during her long sleep. They talked for hours and still had not said half the things they wanted to say to one another.

But the entire palace had woken up with the princess and everyone was going about his business again. Since none of them were in love, they were all dying of hunger. The chief lady-in-waiting, just as ravenous as the rest, lost patience after a while and told the princess loud and clear that dinner was ready. The prince helped the princess up from the bed and she dressed herself with the greatest magnificence; but when she put on her ruff, the prince remembered how his grandmother had worn one just like it. All the princess' clothes were a hundred years out of fashion, but she was no less beautiful because of that.

Supper was served in the hall of mirrors, while the court orchestra played old tunes on violins and oboes they had not touched for a hundred years. After supper, the chaplain married them in the castle chapel and the chief lady-in-waiting drew the curtains round their bed for them. They did not sleep much, that night; the princess did not feel in the least drowsy. The prince left her in the morning, to return to his father's palace.

The king was anxious because his son had been away so long. The prince told him that he had lost himself in the forest while he was out hunting and had spent the night in a charcoal burner's hut, where his host had given him black bread and cheese to eat. The king believed the story but the queen, the prince's mother, was not so easily hoodwinked when she saw that now the young man spent most of his time out hunting in the forest. Though he always arrived back with an excellent excuse when he had spent two or three nights away from home, his mother soon guessed he was in love.

He lived with the princess for more than two years and he gave her two children. They named the eldest, a daughter, Dawn, because she was so beautiful but they called their little son Day because he came after Dawn and was even more beautiful still.

The queen tried to persuade her son to tell her his secret but he dared not confide in her. Although he loved her, he feared her, because she came from a family of ogres and his father had married her only because she was very, very rich. The court whispered that the queen still had ogrish tastes and could hardly keep her hands off little children, so the prince thought it best to say nothing about his own babies.

But when the king died and the prince himself became king, he felt confident enough to publicly announce his marriage and install the new queen, his wife, in his royal palace with a great deal of ceremony. And soon after that, the new king decided to declare war on his neighbour, the Emperor Cantalabutte.

He left the governing of his kingdom in his mother's hands and he trusted her to look after his wife and children for him, too, because he would be away at war for the whole summer.

As soon as he was gone, the queen mother sent her daughter-in-law and her grandchildren away to the country, to a house deep in the woods, so that she could satisfy her hideous appetites with the greatest of ease. She herself arrived at the house a few days later and said to the butler:

"I want to eat little Dawn for my dinner tomorrow."

"Oh, my lady!" exclaimed the butler.

"She's just the very thing I fancy," said the queen mother in the voice of an ogress famished for fresh meat. "And I want you to serve her up with sauce Robert."

The poor man saw he could not argue with a hungry ogress, picked up a carving knife and went to little Dawn's room. She was just four years old. When she saw her dear friend, the butler, she ran up to him, laughing, threw her arms around his neck and asked him where her sweeties were. He burst into tears and the knife fell from his hands. He went down to the farmyard and slaughtered a little lamb instead. He served the lamb up in such a delicious sauce the queen mother said she had never eaten so well in her life and he spirited little Dawn away from harm; he handed her over to his wife, who hid her in a cellar, in the servants' quarters.

Eight days passed. Then the ogress said to the butler:

"I want to eat little Day for my supper."

The butler was determined to outwit her again. He found little Day playing at fencing with his pet monkey; the child was only three. He took him to his wife, who hid him away with his sister, and served up a tender young kid in his place. The queen mother smacked her lips over the dish, so all went well until the night the wicked ogress said to the butler:

"I want to eat the queen with the same sauce you made for her children."

This time, the poor butler did not know what to do. The queen was twenty, now, if you did not count the hundred years she had been asleep; her skin was white and lovely but it was a little tough, and where in all the farmyard was he to find a beast with skin just like it? There was nothing for it; he must kill the queen to save himself and he went to her room, determined he would not have to enter it a second time. He rushed in with a dagger in his hand and told her her mother-in-law had ordered her to die.

"Be quick about it," she said calmly. "Do as she told you. When I am dead, I shall be with my poor children again, my children whom I love so much."

Because they had been taken away from her without a word of explanation, she thought they were dead.

The butler's heart melted.

"No, no, my lady, you don't need to die so that you can be with your children. I've hidden them away from the queen mother's hunger and I will trick her again, I will give her a young deer for supper instead of you."

He took her to the cellar, where he left her kissing her children and weeping over them, and went to kill a young doe that the queen mother ate for supper with as much relish as if it had been her daughter-in-law. She was very pleased with her own cruelty and practised telling her son how the wolves had eaten his wife and children while he had been away at the wars.

One night as she prowled about as usual, sniffing for the spoor of fresh meat, she heard a voice coming from the servants' quarters. It was little Day's voice; he was crying because he had been naughty and his mother wanted to whip him. Then the queen mother heard Dawn begging her mother to forgive the little boy. The ogress recognised the voices of her grandchildren and she was furious. She ordered a huge vat to be brought into the middle of the courtyard. She had the vat filled with toads, vipers, snakes and serpents and then the queen, her children, the butler, his wife and his maid were brought in front of her with their hands tied behind their backs. She was going to have them thrown into the vat.

The executioners were just on the point of carrying out their dreadful instructions when the king galloped into the courtyard. Nobody had expected him back so soon. He was astonished at what he saw and asked who had commanded the vat and the bonds. The ogress was so angry to see her plans go awry that she jumped head-first into the vat and the vile beasts inside devoured her in an instant. The king could not help grieving a little; after all, she was his mother. But his beautiful wife and children soon made him happy again.

MORAL

A brave, rich, handsome husband is a prize well worth waiting for; but no modern woman would think it was worth waiting for a hundred years. The tale of the Sleeping Beauty shows how long engagements make for happy marriages, but young girls these days want so much to be married I do not have the heart to press the moral.

The Fairies

There once lived an old widow who had two daughters. The eldest was the living image of her mother to look at, and worse, to listen to; they were both so proud and disagreeable it was impossible to live with them. But the youngest took after her father in gentleness and kindness and she was also very, very beautiful. Because it is only natural to love people like oneself, the widow adored her eldest daughter and could scarcely stand the sight of the youngest one, who had to have her meals all by herself in the kitchen while the others ate in the dining room, and she made her slave away at all the household chores, too.

Twice a day, she had to go and fetch water from a spring half a mile from the house and bring home a brimming pitcherful. One day, when she went to the spring, she found an old woman there who begged her for a drink.

"Oh yes, indeed!" said the lovely girl with alacrity. She rinsed out her pitcher and dipped it into the spring just where it bubbled out freshly from the rock; and she held the pitcher carefully so that the old woman could drink from it in comfort.

Now, this old woman was really a fairy who had assumed the form of a poor peasant in order to test the girl's good heart. As soon as she finished her drink, she said:

"You are so beautiful, so good and so kind that I feel I must give you a special present. My fairy gift is this: at each word you say, either a flower or else a precious stone will fall out of your mouth."

When the lovely girl arrived home, how they berated her for staying so long at the fountain!

"Mother, dear, I beg your pardon," said the girl and out of her mouth dropped two roses, two pearls and two fat diamonds.

"What do I see before me?" cried her mother. "I could have sworn I saw pearls and diamonds dropping out of her mouth! What can you have been up to, my dear?"

It was the first time in all her life she'd used an endearment towards her younger daughter. The girl told her mother exactly what had happened, scattering a great many diamonds as she did so.

"I must send my eldest girl to the well at once," said the widow. "Fanchon, just look at what comes out of your sister's mouth whenever she opens it! Wouldn't you like to be the same? All you have to do is to go and fetch the water from the spring and give some to the poor woman who'll ask you for a drink."

"I'd like to see myself going off to the spring like a slavey!" snapped the ugly one.

"Go you shall; and this very minute," her mother snapped back.

So off she went but she grumbled all the way and she would not take a common pitcher but armed herself with the best silver jug in the house. No sooner had she arrived at the spring than a fine lady dressed in the height of fashion came out of the woods and asked if she could drink from her jug. This lady was the very same fairy who had appeared to her sister, but now she put on the manners of a princess in order to find out just how rude Fanchon could be.

"Haven't I dragged myself all the way here just to give you a drink of water?" whined Fanchon. "Haven't I lugged this silver flagon all the way from home expressly for madame's drinking convenience? Oh, yes, that's why I've come; drink, if you want to, you've caused me quite enough bother."

The fairy did not lose her temper.

"Nobody could call you a nice woman," she said coolly. "Since you are so disobliging, I shall disoblige you with a most inconvenient present; every time you say one single word, you'll shed either a toad or a snake from your uncivil lips."

When her mother saw Fanchon coming home, she cried: "How did it go?"

"It's all your fault!" whined the ugly one, and out of her mouth fell two vipers and a pair of toads.

"Heavens above, what do I see?" cried her mother. "Your sister is responsible for this. I'll pay her back!"

She hurried off to find her, to beat her, and the poor child ran away into the neighbouring forest to save herself. The king's son met her as he came home from hunting. When he saw how pretty she was, he asked her what she was doing in the woods all by herself; and why was she crying so?

"Alas, kind sir! My own mother has driven me away from home!"

The prince saw five or six pearls and just as many diamonds come tumbling out of her mouth when she spoke and he begged her to tell him where they came from. She told him everything.

The prince was charmed with her and decided that her remarkable talent was worth more than the dowry of any princess in the world; he took her to the palace of the king, his father, and married her.

Her sister grew so hateful that even her mother got tired of her, at last, and turned her out of doors. Try as she might, she could find nobody to take pity on her and she crept away and died in a corner of the woods.

MORAL

Kindness and consideration for others may inconvenience one, in the short run; but, sooner or later, kindness reaps its rewards and often when least expected.

ANOTHER MORAL

Diamonds and pearls make powerful impressions; but kind words are more powerful still, and are infinitely more valuable.

Cinderella: or, The Little Glass Slipper

There once lived a man who married twice, and his second wife was the haughtiest and most stuck-up woman in the world. She already had two daughters of her own and her children took after her in every way. Her new husband's first wife had given him a daughter of his own before she died, but she was a lovely and sweet-natured girl, very like her own natural mother, who had been a kind and gentle woman.

The second wedding was hardly over before the step-mother showed her true colours. Her new daughter was so lovable that she made her own children seem even more unpleasant, by contrast; so she found the girl insufferable. She gave her all the rough work about the house to do, washing the pots and pans, cleaning out Madame's bedroom and those of her step-sisters, too. She slept at the top of the house, in a garret, on a thin, lumpy mattress, while her step-sisters had rooms with fitted carpets, soft beds and mirrors in which they could see themselves from head to foot. The poor girl bore everything patiently and dared not complain to her father because he would have lost his temper with her. His new wife ruled him with a rod of iron.

When the housework was all done, she would tuck herself away in the chimney corner to sit quietly among the cinders, the only place of privacy she could find, and so the family nicknamed her Cinderbritches. But the younger sister, who was less spiteful than the older one, changed her nickname to Cinderella. Yet even in her dirty clothes, Cinderella could not help but be a hundred times more beautiful than her sisters, however magnificently they dressed themselves up.

The king's son decided to hold a ball to which he invited all the aristocracy. Our two young ladies received their invitations, for they were well connected. Busy and happy, they set about choosing the dresses and hairstyles that would suit them best and that made more work for Cinderella, who had to iron her sisters' petticoats and starch their ruffles. They could talk about nothing except what they were going to wear.

"I shall wear my red velvet with the lace trimming," said the eldest.

"Well, I shall wear just a simple skirt but put my coat with the golden flowers over it and, of course, there's always my diamond necklace, which is really rather special," said the youngest.

They sent for a good hairdresser to cut and curl their hair and they bought the best cosmetics. They called Cinderella to ask for her advice, because she had excellent taste. Cinderella helped them to look as pretty as they could and they were very glad of her assistance, although they did not show it.

As she was combing their hair, they said to her:

"Cinderella, dear, wouldn't you like to go to the ball yourself?"

"Oh, don't make fun of me, my ladies, how could I possibly go to the ball!"

"Quite right, too; everyone would laugh themselves silly to see Cinderbritches at a ball."

Any other girl but Cinderella would have made horrid tangles of their hair after that, out of spite; but she was kind, and resisted the temptation. The step-sisters could not eat for two days, they were so excited. They broke more than a dozen corset-laces because they pulled them in so tightly in order to make themselves look slender and they were always primping in front of the mirror.

At last the great day arrived. When they went off, Cinderella watched them until they were out of sight and then began to cry. Her godmother saw how she was crying and asked her what the matter was.

"I want . . . I want to . . ."

But Cinderella was crying so hard she could not get the words out.

Her godmother was a fairy. She said: "I think you're crying because you want to go to the ball."

"Yes," said Cinderella, sighing.

"If you are a good girl, I'll send you there," said her godmother.

She took her into her own room and said:

"Go into the garden and pick me a pumpkin."

Cinderella went out to the garden and picked the finest pumpkin she could find. She took it to her godmother, although she could not imagine how a pumpkin was going to help her get to the ball. Her godmother hollowed out the pumpkin until there was nothing left but the shell, struck it with her ring—and instantly the pumpkin changed into a beautiful golden coach.

Then the godmother went to look in the mousetrap, and found six live mice there. She told Cinderella to lift up the lid of the trap enough to let the mice come out one by one and, as each mouse crept out, she struck it lightly with her ring. At the touch of the ring, each mouse changed into a carriage horse. Soon the coach had six dappled greys to draw it.

Then she asked herself what would do for a coachman.

"I'll go and see if there is a rat in the rat-trap," said Cinderella. "A rat would make a splendid coachman."

"Yes, indeed," said her godmother. "Go and see."

There were three fat rats in the rat-trap that Cinderella brought to her. One had particularly fine whiskers, so the godmother chose that one; when she struck him with her ring, he changed into a plump coachman who had the most imposing moustache you could wish to see.

"If you look behind the watering-can in the garden, you'll find six lizards," the godmother told Cinderella. "Bring them to me."

No sooner had Cinderella brought them to her godmother than the lizards were all changed into footmen, who stepped up behind the carriage in their laced uniforms and hung on as if they had done nothing else all their lives.

The fairy said to Cinderella:

"There you are! Now you can go to the ball. Aren't you pleased?"

"Yes, of course. But how can I possibly go to the ball in these wretched rags?"

The godmother had only to touch her with her ring and Cinderella's workaday overalls and apron changed into a dress of cloth of gold and silver, embroidered with precious stones. Then she gave her the prettiest pair of glass slippers. Now Cinderella was ready, she climbed into the coach; but her godmother told her she must be home by midnight because if she stayed at the ball one moment more, her coach would turn back into a pumpkin, her horses to mice, her footmen to lizards and her clothes back into overalls again.

She promised her godmother that she would be sure to return from the ball before midnight. Then she drove off.

The king's son had been told that a great princess, hitherto unknown to anyone present, was about to arrive at the ball and ran to receive her. He himself helped her down from her carriage with his royal hand and led her into the ballroom where all the guests were assembled. As soon as they saw her, an enormous silence descended. The dancing ceased, the fiddlers forgot to ply their bows as the entire company gazed at this unknown lady. The only sound in the entire ballroom was a confused murmur:

"Oh, isn't she beautiful!"

Even the king himself, although he was an old man, could not help gazing at her and remarked to the queen that he had not seen such a lovely young lady for a long time. All the women studied her hair and her ball-gown attentively so that they would be able to copy them the next day, provided they could find such a capable hairdresser, such a skilful dressmaker, such magnificent silk.

The king's son seated her in the most honoured place and then led her on to the dance floor; she danced so gracefully, she was still more admired. Then there was a fine supper but the prince could not eat at all, he was too preoccupied with the young lady. She herself went and sat beside her sisters and devoted herself to entertaining them. She shared the oranges and lemons the prince had given her with them and that surprised them very much, for they did not recognise her.

While they were talking, Cinderella heard the chimes of the clock striking a quarter to twelve. She made a deep curtsey and then ran off as quickly as she could. As soon as she got home, she went to find her godmother and thanked her and told her how much she wanted to go to the ball that was to be given the following day, because the king's son had begged her to. While she was telling her godmother everything that had happened, her step-sisters knocked at the door. Cinderella hurried to let them in.

"What a long time you've been!" she said to them yawning, rubbing her eyes and stretching as if she could scarcely keep awake, although she had not wanted to sleep for a single moment since they had left the house.

"If you had come to the ball, you wouldn't have been sleepy!" said one of the sisters. "The most beautiful princess you ever saw arrived unexpectedly and she was so kind to us, she gave us oranges and lemons."

Cinderella asked the name of the princess but they told her nobody knew it, and the king's son was in great distress and would give anything to find out more about her. Cinderella smiled and said:

"Was she really so very beautiful? Goodness me, how lucky you are. And can I never see her for myself? What a shame! Miss Javotte, lend me that old yellow dress you wear around the house so that I can go to the ball tomorrow and see her for myself."

"What?" exclaimed Javotte. "Lend my dress to such a grubby little Cinderbritches as it is—it must think I've lost my reason!"

Cinderella had expected a refusal; and she would have been exceedingly embarrassed if her sister had relented and agreed to lend her a dress and taken her to the ball in it.

Next day, the sisters went off to the ball again. Cinderella went, too, but this time she was even more beautifully dressed than the first time. The king's son did not leave her side and never stopped paying her compliments so that the young girl was utterly absorbed in him and time passed so quickly that she thought it must still be only eleven o'clock when she heard the chimes of midnight. She sprang to her feet and darted off as lightly as a doe. The prince sprang after her but could not catch her; in her flight, however, she let fall one of her glass slippers and the prince tenderly picked it up. Cinderella arrived home out of breath, without her carriage, without her footmen, in her dirty old clothes again; nothing remained of all her splendour but one of her little slippers, the pair of the one she had dropped. The prince asked the guards at the palace gate if they had seen a princess go out; they replied they had seen nobody leave the castle last night at midnight but a ragged young girl who looked more like a kitchen-maid than a fine lady.

When her sisters came home from the ball, Cinderella asked them if they had enjoyed themselves again; and had the beautiful princess been there? They said, yes; but she had fled at the very stroke of midnight, and so promptly that she had dropped one of her little glass slippers. The king's son had found it and never took his eyes off it for the rest of the evening, so plainly he was very much in love with the beautiful young lady to whom it belonged.

They spoke the truth. A few days later, the king's son publicly announced that he would marry whoever possessed the foot for which the glass slipper had been made. They made a start by trying the slipper on the feet of all the princesses; then moved on to the duchesses, then to the rest of the court, but all in vain. At last they brought the slipper to the two sisters, who did all they could to squeeze their feet into the slipper but could not manage it, no matter how hard they tried. Cinderella watched them; she recognised her own slipper at once. She laughed, and said:

"I'd like to try and see if it might not fit me!"

Her sisters giggled and made fun of her but the gentleman who was in charge of the slipper trial looked at Cinderella carefully and saw how beautiful she was. Yes, he said; of course she could try on the slipper. He had received orders to try the slipper on the feet of every girl in the kingdom. He sat Cinderella down and, as soon as he saw her foot, he knew it would fit the slipper perfectly. The two sisters were very much astonished but not half so astonished as they were when Cinderella took her own glass slipper from her pocket. At that the godmother appeared; she struck Cinderella's overalls with her ring and at once the old clothes were transformed to garments more magnificent than all her ball-dresses.

Then her sisters knew she had been the beautiful lady they had seen at the ball. They threw themselves at her feet to beg her to forgive them for all the bad treatment she had received from them. Cinderella raised them up and kissed them and said she forgave them with all her heart and wanted them only always to love her. Then, dressed in splendour, she was taken to the prince. He thought she was more beautiful than ever and married her a few days later. Cinderella, who was as good as she was beautiful, took her sisters to live in the palace and arranged for both of them to be married, on the same day, to great lords.

MORAL

Beauty is a fine thing in a woman; it will always be admired. But charm is beyond price and worth more, in the long run. When her godmother dressed Cinderella up and told her how to behave at the ball, she instructed her in charm. Lovely ladies, this gift is worth more than a fancy hairdo; to win a heart, to reach a happy ending, charm is the true gift of the fairies. Without it, one can achieve nothing; with it, everything.

ANOTHER MORAL

It is certainly a great advantage to be intelligent, brave, well-born, sensible and have other similar talents given only by heaven. But however great may be your god-given store, they will never help you to get on in the world unless you have either a godfather or a godmother to put them to work for you.

Ricky with the Tuft

There was once a queen who gave birth to a son so ugly and ungainly that even his mother's heart could not warm to him at all. But the fairy midwife who attended her told her she would certainly learn to love him because he would grow up to be very clever and exceptionally charming and, she added, because of the gift she was about to make him, he would be able to share his native wit with the one he would love best, when the time came.

So the queen was somewhat consoled for having brought such an ugly object into the world and no sooner had the child learned to speak than he began to chatter away so cleverly, and to behave with so much engaging intelligence, that everyone was charmed by him and he was universally loved. I forgot to tell you that he was born with a little tuft of hair on top of his head, which earned him the nickname: Ricky with the Tuft. Ricky was the name of his family.

At the end of seven or eight years, the queen of a neighbouring country gave birth to twin daughters. The first to be born was as beautiful as the day; the queen was so overjoyed that the nurses were afraid she might lose her senses. The same fairy midwife who had attended the birth of Ricky with the Tuft had arrived to look after this queen, too, and, to calm her excesses, she told her that, alas, the pretty little princess had no sense at all and would grow up to be as stupid as she was beautiful. The queen was very upset to hear that and even more upset, a moment or two later, when her second daughter arrived in the world and *this* one proved to be extraordinarily ugly.

"Don't distress yourself, madame," said the fairy. "Your other daughter will have many compensations. She will be so clever and witty that nobody will notice how plain she is."

"I truly hope so!" exclaimed the queen. "But isn't there any way we could give this pretty one just a spark or two of the ugly one's wit?"

"I can do nothing for her on that account," said the fairy. "But I can certainly make her more beautiful than any girl in the world. And since there is nothing I would not do to make you happy, I am going to give her the power to make whoever it is with whom she falls in love as beautiful as she is, too."

As the two princesses grew up, their perfections grew with them and everywhere nobody talked of anything but the beauty of the elder and the wit and wisdom of the younger. But age also emphasised their defects. The younger grew more ugly as you looked at her and the elder became daily more and more stupid. Either she was struck dumb the minute somebody spoke to her or else she said something very foolish in reply. Besides, she was so clumsy she could not put four pots on the mantelpiece without spilling half of it on her clothes.

Although beauty is usually a great asset in a young woman, her younger sister always far outshone the elder in company. First of all, they would flock around the lovely one to look at her and admire her but soon she was abandoned for the company of the one with more to say for herself. And in less than a quarter of an hour, there she would be, all by herself and the younger the centre of an animated throng. However stupid the elder might be, she could not help but notice it and she would have sacrificed all her beauty without a single regret for half her sister's wit, intelligence and charm. The queen tried to prevent herself but, even so, she could not help reproach the girl for her stupidity now and then and that made the poor princess want to die for grief.

One day, when she was hiding herself in a wood bemoaning her fate, she saw a little man whose unprepossessing appearance was equalled only by the magnificence of his clothes. It was the young prince, Ricky with the Tuft, who had fallen head over heels in love with the pretty pictures of the princess that were on sale in all the shops. He had left his father's kingdom in order to see her in the flesh, and speak to her. He was delighted to meet her accidentally, alone in the wood, and greeted her with great respect. After he had paid her the usual compliments, he saw how sad she looked and said to her:

"Madame, I don't understand how a lady as beautiful as you are could possibly be as unhappy as you seem to be. I've had the good fortune to meet a great many beautiful people but I can truthfully say I've never seen anybody half as beautiful as you."

"You are very kind," said the princess and, since she could think of nothing more to say, she fell abruptly silent.

"Beauty is such a blessing, why! it is more important than anything," said Ricky. "And if one is beautiful, I don't understand how anything could ever upset one."

"Oh, I'd much rather be as ugly as you are and be clever than be as beautiful and as terribly, terribly stupid as me!"

"Nothing reveals true wisdom so much as the conviction one is a fool, madame; and the truly wise are those who know they are fools."

"I don't know anything about any of that," said the princess. "But I do know I really am a fool and that's the reason why I'm so unhappy."

"If that's the only reason for your unhappiness, madame, then I can cure it in a trice."

"How can you do that?" asked the princess.

"Well, madame, I have the power to dower the lady whom I love with as much wit as she wishes and, since you are the very one for me, wit and wisdom are yours for the asking if you would consent to become my wife."

The princess was utterly taken aback and could not speak a single word.

"I see my proposal throws you into a state of confusion," said Ricky with the Tuft. "That doesn't surprise me. I will give you a whole year in which to make up your mind."

The princess had so few brains and such a longing to possess some that she imagined a year would be endless so she accepted his proposal on the spot. No sooner had she promised Ricky with the Tuft that she would marry him that same day in one year's time than she felt a great change come over her. From that moment, she began such a brilliant and witty conversation with Ricky that he thought he must have given her more intelligence than he had kept for himself.

When she went home to the palace, the courtiers did not know what to think of the sudden and extraordinary change in her. Before, she had babbled idiocies; now she said the wisest things, and always with a sweet touch of wit. Everyone was overjoyed, except her younger sister whose nose was put sadly out of joint because, now she no longer outshone her sister in conversation, nothing detracted from her ugliness and she looked the plain little thing she really was beside her.

The king took advice from his counsellors. The news of the change in the princess was publicly announced and all the young princes from the neighbouring kingdoms tried to make her fall in love with them. But she found that not one of them was half as clever as she was and she listened to all their protestations unmoved. However, at last there came a prince so powerful, so rich and so handsome that she felt her interest quicken slightly. Her father told her that she could choose her own husband from among her suitors. She thanked him and asked him for a little time in which to decide.

So that she could make up her mind in peace she went off for a walk by herself and, by chance, she found herself in the same wood where she had met Ricky with the Tuft. As she walked through the wood, deep in thought, she heard a noise under her feet, as if a great many people were coming and going, hither and thither, in a great bustle, underground. Listening attentively, she thought she heard a voice demand: "Bring me that roasting pan," and another say: "Fetch me the saucepan," and yet another cry: "Put a bit more wood on the fire." Then the very ground opened in front of her and she saw a huge kitchen full of cooks, scullions and all the staff required to prepare a magnificent banquet. Out of the kitchen came a band of twenty or thirty spit-turners who at once took up their positions round a long table and, chef's caps on the sides of their heads, larding needles in hand, all went busily to work, singing away.

The princess was astonished at the spectacle and asked them who was their master.

"Why, Prince Ricky with the Tuft, madame," replied the head cook. "And tomorrow is his wedding day."

The princess was more surprised than ever. Then, in a flash, she remembered how, just a year before, she had promised to marry Ricky with the Tuft; and when she remembered that, she thought she would faint. She had forgotten her promise completely. When she had said she would marry Ricky, she had been a fool and, as soon as she possessed all the sense the prince had given her, her earlier follies had vanished from her mind.

In a state of some agitation, she walked on but she had not gone thirty paces before Ricky with the Tuft presented himself to her, dressed like a prince on his wedding day.

"See, madame!" he said. "I have come to keep my word and I do not doubt that you are here in order to keep yours."

"I must confess to you that I have not made up my mind on that point," answered the princess, "and I fear that I do not think I shall ever be able to do as you wish."

"You astonish me, madame," said Ricky with the Tuft.

"I daresay I do," said the princess calmly. "And, certainly, if I were dealing with an insensitive man, I should feel very embarrassed. An insensitive man would say to me: 'A princess must keep her word. You promised to marry me and marry me you shall.' But I know I am speaking to a subtle and perceptive man of the world and I am certain he will listen to reason. As you know, when I was a fool, I could not bring myself to a firm decision concerning our marriage. Now I have the brains you gave me, I am even more difficult to please than I was then. And would you wish me to make a decision today that I could not make when I had no sense? If you wished to marry me, you did me a great wrong to take away my stupidity and make me see clearly things I never saw before."

Ricky with the Tuft replied:

"If an insensitive man would be justified in reproaching you for breaking your word, why should you expect, madame, that I should not behave in the same way when my whole life's happiness is at stake? Is it reasonable that a sensitive man should be treated worse than an insensitive one? Would you say that, when you possess so much reason yourself, and wanted it so much? But let us come to the point. With the single exception of my ugliness, is there anything in me that displeases you? Are you dissatisfied with my birth, my intelligence, my personality or my behaviour?"

"Not at all," replied the princess. "I love everything about you except your person."

"If that is so, then I am going to be very happy," said Ricky with the Tuft. "For you alone can make me the handsomest of men."

"How can I do that?" asked the princess.

"By loving me enough to make it come true," said Ricky. "The fairy midwife who gave me the power to make the one I loved wise and witty also gave you the power to make the one you love as beautiful as you are yourself, if you truly wish it so."

"If that is the way of things," said the princess, "I wish with all my heart that you may become the handsomest prince in all the world."

As soon as she said that, Ricky with the Tuft seemed to her the handsomest man she had ever seen.

But some people say there was no magic involved in this transformation and love alone performed the miracle. They whispered that when the princess took into account her lover's faithfulness, his sense, his good qualities, and his intellect, then she no longer saw how warped his body was nor how ugly his face. His hump seemed to her no more than good, broad shoulders; at first she thought he had a frightful limp but now she saw it was really a charming, scholarly stoop. His eyes only sparkled the more because of his squint and she knew that squint was due to the violence of his passion. And how martial, how heroic, she thought his huge, red nose was!

Be that as it may, the princess promised to marry him there and then, provided he obtained consent of the king, her father.

The king saw how much in love his daughter was with Ricky with the Tuft and, besides, he knew him for a wise and prudent prince. He accepted him as his son-in-law with pleasure.

The next day, the wedding was celebrated just as Ricky had foreseen, according to the arrangements he had made a year before.

MORAL

This is not a fairy tale but the plain, unvarnished truth; every feature of the face of the one we love is beautiful, every word the beloved says is wise.

ANOTHER MORAL

A beautiful soul is one thing, a beautiful face another. But love alone can touch the heart.

Hop o' my Thumb

A certain woodcutter and his wife were blessed with seven sons. The eldest was ten years old and the youngest seven. It may seem a remarkable feat to produce so many children in so little time but the woodcutter's wife had gone to work with a will and rarely given her husband less than two at once.

They were very poor and their seven children were a great inconvenience because none of them could earn their living.

The youngest was the greatest inconvenience of all; he was a weakling and a mute, and they mistook his debility for stupidity. He was very, very tiny and when he came into the world he was scarcely bigger than your thumb. So they called him "Hop o' my Thumb".

This poor child was the butt of the household and they were always finding fault with him. But he was really the cleverest of them all and if he did not speak much, he listened very, very carefully.

At last there came a year of such terrible famine that the poor people decided they could not provide for their children any more.

One evening, when the children were in bed and the woodcutter sat with his wife by the fire, he said to her with a breaking heart:

"You know we've got nothing to give our children to eat. I can't bear to see them die of hunger in front of my very eyes. I've decided to take them out in the woods tomorrow and lose them there. It will be very easy. While they are gathering up sticks, we'll slip away without them seeing us."

"Oh!" cried his wife. "How could you think of abandoning your own children?"

Her husband painted a grisly picture of their plight but, all the same, she would not agree to his scheme—she was poor, but she was their mother. But then when she thought how sad she would be to see them starve to death, she said, yes; and went to bed in tears.

When Hop o' my Thumb had realised his parents were discussing something of importance, he crept from his bed and hid himself under his father's stool, to eavesdrop, so he heard everything they said. Back he went to bed but he did not sleep that night; he was planning his strategy. He got up early and went to the bank of a stream, and filled his pockets with little white pebbles. Then he came home again. When the family set off for the wood, Hop o' my Thumb did not tell his brothers his dreadful secret.

They went to the thickest part of the forest, where you could not see another person if you were ten steps away from them. The woodcutter began to chop down a tree and the children went off to collect sticks and make them up into bundles. When their father and mother saw they were busy and happy, they edged further and further away, until they could no longer glimpse a single child: then they took to their heels and fled.

When the children found out they were all by themselves, they began to cry with all their might. Hop o' my Thumb let them cry for a while, because he knew how to get back home again. As they walked through the forest, he had let drop the little white pebbles he had kept in his pocket all along the way. Now he said to his brothers:

"Don't be scared. Mother and father have abandoned us here, but I will take you home again. Just follow me."

They trooped after him and he led them straight home by the same way they had gone into the forest. At first, they did not dare go inside the cottage, but listened at the door to find out what was going on.

As soon as the woodcutter and his wife had arrived home, the village squire sent them ten golden sovereigns he had owed them for so long they had given up hope he would ever repay the debt. The money was life to them; they were dying of hunger. The woodcutter sent his wife straight out to the butcher's. They had not eaten for so long she had forgotten how much meat to buy and bought three times as much as the two of them needed. When they sat down at table, the woodcutter's wife lamented:

"Alas, where are our poor children now? They would have feasted off the leavings of our spread! But you would insist in getting rid of them, William; I told you we would regret it. What are they doing in the forest? Perhaps the wolves have already eaten them! What an inhuman brute you are, to abandon your children!"

If she reminded him once she reminded him twenty times how he'd regret it and at last he lost patience with her and threatened to beat her if she did not keep quiet. She was making a deafening clamour and he was the kind of man who likes a woman to speak her mind but can't stand a woman who is always right.

The woodcutter's wife was crying dreadfully.

"Alas, alas, where are my poor children?"

She cried so loudly that the children outside heard her and sang out all together:

"Here we are! Here we are!"

She ran to open the door for them and hugged and kissed them.

"Oh, my darlings, how happy I am to see you! You must be very tired, you must be very hungry . . . Oh, Pierrot! How dirty you are! Come and have your face washed!"

Pierrot was her eldest son and she loved him more than all the others because he had ginger hair and her own hair was on the carroty side, too.

They sat down and ate so much their mother and father were filled with joy. They told their parents how scary the forest had been, interrupting one another and all talking at once. The woodcutter and his wife were delighted to have their children home with them and the joy lasted exactly as long as the ten golden sovereigns. But when the money was all gone, they began to despair and decided, once again, to leave the children to their fates. But this time there would be no mistake. They would take the children twice as far from home before they abandoned them, so they could never return.

But they could not plot secretly enough to stop Hop o' my Thumb hearing them and he made it his business to organise things as he had done before. But when he got up at dawn to go and fetch his pebbles, his scheme came to nothing, for he found the door of the house securely locked. He did not know what to do until the woodcutter's wife gave each of them a piece of bread for their lunch.

Then he thought he would be able to use breadcrumbs instead of pebbles to scatter behind him along the way, so he stored his bread in his pocket.

Their father and mother took them to the densest, darkest part of the forest and once they had arrived, they slipped away through the undergrowth and left the children behind. Hop o' my Thumb did not worry very much, at first, because he thought he could easily find his way home because of the track of breadcrumbs he had scattered as he walked; but he was astonished to discover he could not find a single crumb when he started to look for them, because the birds had come and eaten them all.

Now they were in a sorry state. The more they searched for the way home, the more they lost themselves in the forest. Night came on and brought a great wind with it, so they were very much afraid. They thought they heard the howling of wolves who had come to devour them. They hardly dared speak. Then it began to rain and they were soaked through. They slithered in the mud at every step, fell down and dragged themselves to their feet again, filthy from head to toe.

Hop o' my Thumb climbed up a tree to see if he could discover anything about their surroundings. He looked about on all sides until he saw a little glimmer of light like the light from a candle, far off in the forest. When he came down from his perch, he could see nothing but he made his brothers trudge off in the direction of the light and, after a while, they saw it again as they came out of the wood.

At last they arrived at the house with the candle in the window, not without more alarms—they often lost sight of the light and fell into holes several times. They knocked at the door and a woman answered it. She asked them what they wanted.

"We are poor children lost in the forest," replied Hop o' my Thumb. "Can we beg a bed for the night, in the name of charity?"

The woman saw how pretty they were and began to weep.

"Oh, you poor children, why have you come? Don't you know who lives here? A horrid ogre, who eats babies."

Hop o' my Thumb shook with fear, like his brothers, but he said:

"Oh, kind lady, what shall we do? If you don't let us into your house, the wolves in the forest will certainly eat us. And on the whole, we would very much rather be eaten by the ogre than by the wolves, because the ogre might take pity on us, especially if we ask him to."

The ogre's wife thought she would be able to hide them until the next morning, so she let them in and took them to warm themselves beside a good fire where a whole sheep was turning on a spit for the ogre's supper.

While they were thawing out, they heard three or four great bangs at the door; the ogre had come home. The ogre's wife hid them under the bed and went to let him in. The ogre asked if his supper was ready and his wine drawn from the barrel; then he sat down at the table. The sheep was still turning on the spit but he thought he smelled something better than roast mutton. He snuffed the air to the right and he snuffed the air to the left; he said he smelled fresh meat.

"Why, that must be the calf I was just going to skin!" said his wife.

"I smell fresh meat, I tell you," repeated the ogre, looking at his wife suspiciously. "And something is going on that I don't understand."

He got up and went straight to the bed.

"So you wanted to trick me, did you, you old cow! I don't know why I don't eat you, too, but I daresay you'd be too tough. Here's some game delivered to me at just the right time—the very thing to give my three ogrish friends for dinner tomorrow!"

One after the other, he pulled the poor children from under the bed. They fell to their knees and begged his pardon but they had fallen into the hands of the cruellest of ogres, who, far from taking pity on them, was already eating them up with his eyes and telling his wife they were such delicious morsels that she would have to make an especially good sauce to go with them.

He got out an enormous knife and began to sharpen it on a long stone, under the terrified gaze of Hop o' my Thumb and his brothers. But when he seized hold of Pierrot, his wife said:

"What can you be thinking of, slaughtering at this hour? Won't there be enough time tomorrow?"

"Keep your mouth shut, you," said the ogre. "I like my game well hung."

"But goodness me, isn't there enough meat in the house already? There's a calf, two sheep and the best part of a pig."

"Oh, very well, then," said the ogre. "Give them some supper to fatten them up and put them to bed."

The ogre's wife was overjoyed and took them plenty of supper but they were too frightened to eat it. As for the ogre, he sat down to some serious drinking to celebrate his pleasure at finding such delicious fare with which to entertain his friends. He put away twice as much good wine as usual and it went to his head, so he stretched out on his bed for a nap.

The ogre had seven little daughters who all had wonderfully fresh complexions because they ate so much fresh meat, just like their father. But besides their rosy cheeks, they had nasty little round grey eyes, hooked noses and enormous mouths with long teeth sharpened to a point, and those teeth had huge gaps between them. They were still too young to be very wicked but they showed signs of great promise and had already taken to biting babies in order to suck their blood.

The horrid little things had all been sent to bed early and were lying, all seven, in one bed, and each wore a golden crown on her head. There was another bed just the same size in their room and the ogre's wife put the seven boys to sleep in it before she went to lie down beside her husband.

Hop o' my Thumb saw the golden crowns on the heads of the little ogresses. He was afraid the ogre might wake up in the night and want to get on with his butchering; after a while, Hop o' my Thumb got up and took the caps off the heads of his brothers. He crept across the room and took the crowns from the heads of the baby ogresses. He put the crowns on his brothers' heads and one on his own, and put their caps on the baby ogresses, so that the ogre would think the woodcutter's sons were his own daughters and the girls were really the boys.

About midnight, the ogre woke up and was seized with regret that he had left till the morrow a task he might have performed that day. He jumped out of bed and picked up his big knife.

"Let's go and have another look at those funny little objects," he said to himself.

He tiptoed into his daughters' bedroom and went to the bed where the little boys slept soundly, except for Hop o' my Thumb, who was very frightened when the ogre's hands groped at his face. But when the ogre touched the golden crown he wore, he said:

"Why, what a nasty trick I almost played on myself! I must have had a drop too much last night."

So off he went to the other bed and felt for the boys' caps.

"Here they are, the little lambs!" he cried. "Let's fall to work."

With that, he slit the throats of his seven daughters. Well content with the night's work, he went back to bed again.

As soon as Hop o' my Thumb heard the ogre start to snore, he woke up his brothers and told them to put their clothes on and follow him. They went into the garden as quietly as they could and jumped over the wall. Shaking with terror, they ran through the night without even knowing where they were going.

When the ogre woke up in the morning, he said to his wife:

"Go down below and get those little fellows from last night ready."

The ogre's wife was surprised and pleased because she thought he meant "get them ready for the day", not "get them ready for the pot". She thought he had taken pity on them. So upstairs she went, and found her seven daughters, with their throats cut, swimming in blood.

She responded with a fainting fit; most women faint in similar circumstances. The ogre thought his wife had been away long enough and climbed up the stairs to see what the matter was.

He was no less astonished than his wife at the spectacle which awaited him.

"What have I done?" he cried. "I'll pay the rascals back for the trick they played me, and pay them back quickly!"

He threw a bucket of water over his wife to bring her round and when she came to he said:

"Quick, get me my seven-league boots so that I can go and catch those criminals!"

He raced across the country until he came to the lane where the poor children were running, and now they were only a hundred yards from their own father's door. They saw the ogre striding from mountain to mountain, and skipping across rivers as if they were streams. Hop o' my Thumb spied a crack in a nearby rock and quickly hid his six brothers there. He tucked himself in beside them, peering out to keep an eye on the ogre. The ogre was weary after his long, useless search; besides, seven-league boots are very exhausting to wear. He wanted a sit down and, as luck would have it, he parked himself on the very rock in which the little boys were hiding.

He was so tired that soon he fell asleep and began to snore so frightfully that the poor children were just as frightened as they had been when he was flourishing his big knife ready to cut their throats. But Hop o' my Thumb told his brothers to run home while the giant was sound asleep and not to bother about him, because he could take care of himself. So off they ran.

Hop o' my Thumb went up to the ogre, took the boots off his feet so gently he did not wake him, and put them on himself. The boots were very long and very large but, since they were of fairy make, they could swell or shrink according to the size of the foot that wore them.

Hop o' my Thumb went to the ogre's house straight away. The ogre's wife was weeping beside the corpses of her daughters.

"Your husband is in terrible danger," announced Hop o' my Thumb. "He has been captured by a gang of robbers who say they will kill him if he doesn't give them all his money. As they held the knife to his throat, he noticed me standing discreetly by and begged me to come straight to you and tell you to give me everything he owns and not keep back a penny. Otherwise, the robbers will kill him without mercy. He told me to borrow his seven-league boots because the matter was so pressing, and to prove to you I was no imposter, too."

The good woman was terrified and quickly gave him all she had, because the ogre was a good husband in spite of his daily diet of young children, and she wanted to save him. Hop o' my Thumb, loaded with the ogre's treasure, took himself off to his father's house, where he had the most joyful welcome.

Some people disagree with this ending—they say that Hop o' my Thumb never robbed the ogre and the truth of it was, that he only took the seven-league boots. These people claim they know the true facts and, to clinch the matter, go so far as to say they have even enjoyed the hospitality of the woodcutter's own home. They say that when Hop o' my Thumb put on the ogre's boots, he went to the king's court because he knew an enemy army was camped two miles away and all at the capital were agog to know the results of the latest battle. They say he went to the king and asked him if he wanted full military reports before sunset. The king promised him a great deal of money for the information and Hop o' my Thumb brought back the news that very evening. After that, the king paid him handsomely to carry orders to the army; besides, a great many ladies paid him any price he cared to name for news of their lovers. He made his greatest profits from this activity.

One or two married women also hired him to send letters to their husbands but they paid very badly and provided very little business; it was a poor thing in comparison.

He worked as a special messenger until he saved up a small fortune. Then he went home to his father's house. He took good care of his entire family; he bought peerages for his father and all his brothers and lived in ease and comfort for the rest of his life.

MORAL

It is no affliction to have a large family if they are all handsome, strong and clever. But if one of them is a puny weakling, he will be despised, jeered at and mocked. However, often the runt of the litter ends up making the family fortune.

The Foolish Wishes

There once lived a woodcutter who was so poor he couldn't enjoy life at all; he thought he was by nature a most unlucky fellow.

One day, at work in the woods, he was moaning away, as usual, when Jupiter, king of the gods, appeared unexpectedly, thunderbolt in hand. The woodcutter was very frightened and threw himself on the ground, apologising profusely for ever having complained about anything at all.

"Don't be scared," said Jupiter. "I'm deeply touched by your misfortunes. Listen. I am the king of the gods and the master of the world. I'm going to grant you three wishes. Anything you want, anything at all, whatever will make you happy—all you have to do is wish for it. But think very carefully before you make your wishes, because they're the only ones you'll ever get."

At that, Jupiter went noisily back to heaven and the woodcutter picked up his bundle of sticks and trudged home, light at heart. "I mustn't wish for anything silly," he said to himself. "Must talk it all over with the wife before I make a decision."

When he reached his cottage, he told his wife, Fanchon, to pile more wood on the fire.

"We're going to be rich!" he said. "All we've got to do is to make three wishes."

He told her what had happened to him and she was dazzled at the prospects that opened up before her. But she thought they should plan their wishes very carefully.

"Blaise, my dear, don't let's spoil everything by being too hasty. Let's talk things over, and put off making our first wish until tomorrow, after we've had a good night's sleep."

"Quite right," said Blaise, her husband. "But let's celebrate; let's have a glass of wine."

She drew some wine from the barrel and he rested his bones in his armchair beside a roaring fire, glass in hand, happier than he had ever been in his life.

"My, oh, my," he said, half to himself. "I know just what would go down well on a night like this; a nice piece of black pudding. Why, I wish I had a piece of black pudding right now!"

No sooner had he spoken these fateful words than Fanchon beheld an enormous black pudding make an unexpected appearance in the chimney corner and come crawling towards her like a snake. First, she screamed; then, when she realised that the black pudding had arrived solely because her stupid husband had made a careless wish, she called him every name under the sun and heaped abuse on his head.

"We could have had an entire empire of our own! Gold and pearls and diamonds and nice clothes, any amount of them—and what do you go and wish for? What's your heart's desire—why, a bit of black pudding!"

"Well, I'm sorry," he said, "What else can I say? I admit it, I've done something very foolish. I'll do better, next time. Haven't I said I'm sorry?"

"Words, words, words," said the woodcutter's wife. "Why don't you go and sleep in the stable; it's the best place for an ass like you."

Her husband lost his temper completely at that and thought how much he'd like to wish to be a widower; but he didn't quite dare say it aloud.

"Men were born to suffer! To hell with the black pudding! I wish that black pudding were hanging from the end of your nose!"

Now, Fanchon was a very pretty woman and nobody would have said her looks were improved by the black pudding but it hung over her mouth and muffled her nagging and, for a single, happy moment, her husband felt he could wish for nothing more.

"After these disasters," he announced, "we must be more prudent. I think I shall use my last remaining wish to make myself a king."

But, all the same, he had to take the queen's feelings into account; how would she like to be a queen and sit on a throne when she had a nose as long as a donkey's? And, because only one wish was left, that was the choice before them—either King Blaise had for his consort the ugliest queen in the world; or they used the wish to get rid of the pudding and Blaise the woodcutter had his pretty wife again.

Fanchon, however, thought there was no choice at all. She wanted her nose in its original condition. Nothing more.

So the woodcutter stayed in his cottage and went out to saw logs every day. He did not become a king; he did not even fill his pockets with money. He was only too glad to use the last wish to make things as they had been again.

MORAL

Greedy, short-sighted, careless, thoughtless, changeable people don't know how to make sensible decisions; and few of us are capable of using well the gifts God gave us, anyway.

Donkey-Skin

Once upon a time, there lived a wise and happy king, who had a beautiful wife, a lovely daughter, a magnificent palace, wise and capable ministers, virtuous and devoted couriers, faithful and hard-working servants and vast stables filled with the finest horses. But everyone who visited those stables was astonished to see how an ugly old donkey with very long ears lolled at its ease in the most sumptuous stall of all. There was more to this beast than met the eye, however; he was well worth all the care the king could give him because, every morning, he covered his litter, not with dung, but with many, many golden coins.

One day, the queen fell sick and no doctor could cure her. The whole country mourned. When she felt her last hour approaching, the queen said to her weeping husband:

"Promise me one thing, before I die; promise me you will marry again."

The king let out a piteous cry, clasped hold of her hands, bathed them with tears and told her he would never so much as think of taking another wife. But the queen said firmly:

"You must and you will marry again. All your ministers will say you must, because I have only given you a daughter and they will say you need sons, to inherit the kingdom. But I beg you, by all the love you have for me, not to marry again until you have found a princess more beautiful than I. Give me your word and I will die happy."

The queen was very vain and did not believe there could possibly be another woman in the world as beautiful as she was, so she thought she had cunningly ensured the king could never marry again at all and died happy. No husband ever made more fuss, weeping, sobbing day and night; but great sorrows do not last long. Besides, all his ministers of state came in a body to see him, just as the queen had said they would, and told him that wedlock was his duty.

The king burst into tears again and reminded them of the promise he had made to the queen, but his ministers said: be that as it may, he owed his country another queen, a live one.

So the king started to look for a suitable fiancée. Every day, he studied charming portraits of suitable princesses but not one of them was half as pretty as his dead queen had been. Then he looked at his own daughter and saw she had grown up. Now she was even lovelier than her mother had been when the king first met her and he fell head over heels in love with her and proposed. The princess was filled with horror. She threw herself at her father's feet and pleaded with him to see reason but the king had set his heart on this strange project, because only by marrying his daughter could he keep the promise he had made to his wife and please his ministers, too. He ordered the girl to obey him.

The young princess decided it was high time she consulted her godmother, the Lilac Fairy, and went off to visit her that very night in a little carriage drawn by a wise sheep who knew all the back alleys of fairyland. The Lilac Fairy, most loving of godmothers, knew already, by magic, what had happened; she told the princess that nothing could harm her if she did what she was told.

"Tell your father you won't marry him unless he gives you a dress that is exactly the colour of the sky. However much he loves you, he will never be able to do that."

The princess thanked her godmother and went home. Next morning, she told her father, the king, that she would not listen to another word from him until he brought her a dress the colour of the sky. The king assembled the finest dressmakers in the kingdom and asked them to make just such a dress. And if they failed, they would be hanged, every one of them.

Next morning, much to the princess' embarrassment, a dress

the very colour of a summer sky full of golden clouds was ready and waiting for her. The king said that now she must marry him; and off she went, again, to her godmother, who told her, this time, to ask for a dress that was the colour of the moon. The king could refuse his darling nothing. He sent for the dressmakers and ordered a dress just like the moon, to be ready in twenty-four hours exactly.

The princess looked at her marvellous new dress, the colour of moonlight, and wept. At that moment, the Lilac Fairy arrived in person to comfort her.

"I think that if you asked for a dress the colour of the sun, we might outwit your father," she said.

So the princess asked for a dress the colour of the sun. The king took all the diamonds and rubies from his crown to ornament this wonderful garment. Nothing was spared; he emptied all his coffers. When the dress was finished, the dressmakers had to shut their eyes, it was so dazzling; that is why dark glasses were invented. The princess had never seen such wonderful workmanship and she was overcome. She said the dress shone so brightly it had given her a headache and retreated to her room, where the Lilac Fairy was waiting for her. The Lilac Fairy was very angry indeed.

"I know your father is quite determined to marry you but I think he would be very stupid indeed if he does as I shall tell you to ask him, now. Ask him for the skin of the donkey who fills his treasury for him. Go at once and ask him."

The princess thought her father would never sacrifice his magic donkey and so she asked for the donkey's skin. The king did not think twice about it; the poor beast was slaughtered that very day and he brought the skin to the princess himself. Now there was no way out. The princess wept and tore her hair but the resourceful Lilac Fairy comforted her.

"Wrap yourself up in the donkey-skin, run away from the palace and go wherever your fortune takes you. God will protect you because you are such a good girl. Off you go; and I will send you your lovely dresses after you. Wherever you may be, your trunk, with all your clothes and jewels in it, will speed after you under the ground. Here! I shall give you my ring. Strike the ground when you need your baggage and there it will be. Now run along quickly, don't dally."

The princess kissed her godmother, wrapped herself in the donkey-skin, smeared her face with soot from the chimney and went out of the palace without anybody recognising her.

The flight of the princess caused a great uproar. The king had already prepared a magnificent wedding and he was in despair. He sent hundreds of soldiers out to search for her but her godmother cast a cloak of invisibility over her so they never found her, and he was left all alone.

The princess went far, very far and then still further, looking for a lodging, but though the village people gave her food, for charity's sake, she was so ugly and dirty nobody would give her a home. At last she came to a fine city and found a farm outside the city gates where the farmer needed a scullery maid, to wash the dishes, feed the turkeys and watch the sheep. When they saw the poor traveller, they asked her in and the princess was glad of it, for she was very tired. She was given a little corner by the kitchen stove where she was the butt of all the jokes of the farm-hands for the first few days, because of her dirty face and the donkey-skin wrapped around her. But they soon got used to her and she did her duties so well the farmer and his wife grew fond of her and took good care of her. Soon she was tending the sheep and turkeys as if she had never done anything else in her life.

For a long time, she never took off her disguise at all but, one day, after she had washed her face and her hands in a little spring and saw how her skin was still fresh and blooming, her hands white and smooth, although she worked so hard, she was so pleased to find she was still beautiful that she washed herself all over. When she was clean again, she could hardly bear to put on her donkey-skin in order to go back to the farm. And, as luck would have it, next day was a holiday and the farm-hands went off to town to enjoy themselves; all was peace and quiet.

In the privacy of her room, she struck the Lilac Fairy's ring on the ground and, in an instant, there stood her trunk with all her dresses in it. She opened her trunk, combed her hair and put on the dress that was the colour of the sky. Her room was so small she could not spread out her blue skirts but, once again, she felt like a real princess.

She decided she would put on all her lovely dresses, turn and turn about, on Sundays and holidays, as her only little treat, and she would put jewels and flowers in her hair, too; and so she did. Every Sunday, every holiday, she would dress herself up and arrange her hair in an elaborate coiffure—and then sigh, because only the sheep and turkeys were there to see how beautiful she was and they loved her just as much when she was wearing the horrid donkey-skin that had earned her the nickname by which she was known at the farm. Donkey-Skin. They called her Donkey-Skin.

One Sunday, when Donkey-Skin happened to have dressed herself up in the dress that was the colour of the sun, the son of the king of that country, who owned the farm, got down from his horse to rest there on his way home from hunting. This prince was young, strong and handsome, the apple of his father's eye. The farmer offered him the best in the house and, after he had eaten and drunk, the prince took a little walk round his property. He came to a dark alley with a door at the end of it and this door was tight shut. Out of curiosity, he bent down and peered through the keyhole. And, in the room, he saw such a beautiful lady in so wonderful a dress she looked like an angel just dropped from heaven. He was so struck with the sight of her he could have forced the door open and rushed inside, if she had not also instantly inspired him with the deepest respect.

He dragged himself away from the dark corner and asked the farmer who it was who lived in the little room. They told him it was the scullery maid, and she was called Donkey-Skin, because of the curious garment she wore, and she was so dirty that nobody could bear to look at her or speak to her. They themselves had only taken her in out of pity, to look after the sheep and the turkeys.

The prince thought there was something very odd about this information but he saw that the farmer and his wife knew nothing more interesting about the girl who lived at the end of the alley and it was useless to question them any further. He went home to the king's palace beside himself with love. He wished he had knocked on the scullery maid's door and swore to himself he would do just that the next time he went to the farm. He was so much in love that he made himself ill; that very night, he was seized with a terrible fever. He was an only child and the queen, his mother, despaired when no medicine seemed to help him. The doctors did all they could but nothing made him any better.

At last, they decided he must have grown sick because of the pangs of an unsatisfied longing. They told the queen their diagnosis and she begged her son to tell her what troubled him. If he wanted to be king, then his father would gladly abdicate in his favour; if he wanted to marry, then they would even go to war to bring home for him the princess he loved. But he must not die, oh, no; for if he died, then his loving parents would die, too, of grief.

"Madame," said the prince weakly, "I am not an unnatural son. I don't want my father's crown; may he live to wear it many years more. As for marriage, I've hardly thought of it."

"Oh, my son, save the lives of your loving parents. Tell me what it is you want and you shall have it."

"What I want most in all the world . . . is that Donkey-Skin should bake me a cake and, when it is ready, she should bring it to me with her own hands."

The queen was startled to hear such an odd name; she asked who Donkey-Skin might be. One of the courtiers had caught sight of the girl at the farm and told the queen:

"It's the ugliest thing in the world, after the wolf. It's a hideous, black, wrinkled object that lives in your farmyard and looks after your turkeys."

"Never mind," said the queen. "Perhaps my son ate some of her cakes on the way back from hunting and now he has a sick fancy to eat them again. Donkey-Skin must bake him a cake immediately."

A messenger ran to the farm and asked Donkey-Skin to bake a cake for the prince as well as she knew how.

Now, some people say that Donkey-Skin saw the prince out of her little window just before he put his eyes to her keyhole, and he was so handsome she could not get him out of her mind. But whether she had seen him, or else had heard the talk about how handsome and brave he was, she was very pleased to find she had the chance to bake a cake for him. She shut herself up in her room, threw off the leathery old pelt, washed her face and hands, combed her golden hair, put on her moon-coloured dress and baked the prince a cake. She used the best flour, eggs and fresh butter. As she worked, either by accident or on purpose, she dropped a ring from her finger into the mixing bowl. When the cake was ready, she wrapped herself up in the donkey-skin again and gave the cake to the messenger. She asked for news of the prince's health but the messenger did not deign to reply; he ran off with the cake straightaway to the palace.

The prince snatched the cake from the messenger's hands and gobbled it so quickly the doctors who were present shook their heads and muttered to themselves about unhealthy appetites. Then he choked on a mouthful and took the princess' ring from his mouth. He stopped devouring the cake and examined his treasure; it was a fine emerald set in such a tiny band of gold that only one finger in the world could have been slender enough to fit it.

He kissed the ring and hid it away under his pillow, though he took it out and looked at it whenever he thought nobody was watching him. He schemed how he could meet the girl whose ring it was but he did not think they would let Donkey-Skin come to see him and he dared not tell anyone what he had seen through the keyhole in case they thought he was delirious. He worried so much that his fever returned and, this time, the doctors diagnosed lovesickness.

The king and queen sat at their son's bedside, weeping.

"Tell us the name of the one you love and, whoever she is, you shall have her," they said.

The prince replied: "Father and mother, there is an emerald ring under my pillow. I want to marry the girl to whom that ring belongs."

The king and queen took the ring, inspected it closely and decided it must belong to a lady. Then the king kissed his son and told him to get well. He ordered drums, pipes and trumpets to play all over the town and heralds to announce that anyone who wanted to try the ring should come to the palace and the girl whose finger it fitted would marry the king's son himself.

First, all the princesses in the kingdom arrived to try it on; then the duchesses, the marchionesses and the peeresses. But though they tugged and pulled at the ring, not one of them had a slender enough finger to wear it. Then they tried it on the seamstresses and though they were all very pretty, their fingers were too big, too. Then came the turn of the chamber-maids, but they had no better luck. At last the prince, who conducted all the trials himself, called for the cooks, the kitchen maids and the shepherdesses and all of them came to try the ring but their hands were so swollen with hard work the ring would not even slip over the first joint of their little fingers.

"Now it is the turn of Donkey-Skin, who baked me a cake when I was sick," said the prince. Everybody burst out laughing and said, no! how could the beautiful ring ever fit Donkey-Skin, who was so ugly and dirty.

"Go and fetch her at once," said the prince. "I mustn't leave anybody out."

Laughing uproariously, they went to fetch the girl who looked after the turkeys.

The princess heard the noise of the drums and the shouts of the heralds and she was very fearful, because she was in love with the prince; true love is humble and she was sure the ring would fit some other lady's finger and she would lose him. When the herald knocked at her door, she was full of joy. She combed her hair and put on her silver bodice with the skirt of silver lace embroidered with emeralds, but she covered all this splendour with her donkey-skin before she left her room. As the messengers from the palace led her to the prince, they mocked her cruelly and when the prince himself saw her in her ugly clothes, he could scarcely believe there might be the same girl inside them whom he had seen through the keyhole at the farm.

"Do you live in a little room at the end of a dark alley behind the farmyard?" he asked her.

"Yes, sir, I do," she replied.

"Show me your hand," he said, trembling.

Out from under that black, hideous hide came a tiny little pink and white hand and the ring slipped smoothly on to her slim finger. The princess shrugged the donkey-skin from her shoulders and there she stood in all her glory, so beautiful that the prince fell at her feet and embraced her knees with an ardour that made her blush. The king and the queen asked her if she would like to marry their son and kissed her, too. The princess was overwhelmed and, as she stammered her thanks, the ceiling of the room opened and down came the Lilac Fairy in a chariot made of branches of lilac, and the Lilac Fairy told them the whole story of how the princess came to wear the donkey-skin.

The king and the queen were naturally delighted to learn that Donkey-Skin was a great princess and the prince loved her still more when he realised how resolute she was. He wanted to marry her so badly he could hardly wait for the banns to be called and his father and mother already adored her. But the princess declared that she could not marry the prince until she had the consent of her own father and so, according to the advice of the Lilac Fairy, who attended to everything, her father was sent a wedding invitation that did not give the name of the bride.

Kings from all over the world came to the wedding, some in sedan chairs, some in carriages. Those from furthest away arrived on elephants, on tigers or on eagles. But the greatest and most magnificent of all the kings was the father of our princess and he had mercifully quite forgotten how he had ever wanted to marry her himself. Indeed, in the meantime, he had married the lovely widow of a neighbouring king. The princess ran to meet him. He recognised her immediately and kissed her very tenderly before she had a chance to kneel before him. He gladly gave his consent to her marriage and the wedding was celebrated with all the pomp imaginable.

The king abdicated that same day and gave his throne to his son, in spite of the young man's protests. The wedding celebrations lasted for three whole months but the love of the married couple lasted longer than that—until they died.

MORAL

The story of Donkey-Skin is not something you might read every day in the morning papers. But as long as there are children, mothers, grandmothers and Mother Goose, it will always seem new.

Afterword

When Charles Perrault first wrote down these fairy tales in the last years of the seventeenth century, they had already existed, in one form or another, for years, some for centuries, part of the unwritten tradition of folk-lore handed down by word of mouth from one generation to another. In France at the time, nursery tales like these were called "Mother Goose Tales"—*Contes de ma Mère l'Oye*—though Mother Goose herself bore no relation to any real person, but was a collective name for every granny, nanny or old wife who ever kept children content with stories about unfortunate princesses, talking beasts or seven-league boots.

As he tells us himself in his *Memoirs,* Charles Perrault was born in Paris, the son of a barrister, on January 12th 1628. At nine years old, he went to school, to the Collège de Beauvais, where he argued with his philosophy teacher so bitterly—claiming his own arguments were superior because "they were new"—that he and a friend finally abandoned formal schooling altogether and adjourned to the garden of the Luxembourg, where they embarked on a course of study directed by themselves.

Perrault was always to do those things best that he had not been trained for; he was the very type of the professional amateur and a literary immortality, based on a book of fairy tales he did not even publish under his own name, was one of the fortunate accidents with which his life abounded.

In 1651 he took a degree in law at Lyons, a place where academic standards were honoured only in name, but soon tired of the legal profession and took a job with his brother, Pierre, the receiver-general of the finances of Paris. During the ten years he spent in this post, he occupied himself writing verses until, in 1657, he directed the construction of a house for his brother and showed such taste and skill in the doing of it that he was eventually employed as secretary to the great statesman, Jean Baptiste Colbert. As Colbert's secretary he had particular concern for the arts and sciences and soon took special responsibility in the department of public works. So Perrault became a senior civil servant and selected the team that designed Versailles and the Louvre. The principal architect of the Louvre was another brother, Claude, by profession a physician. Perrault had some of the healthy opportunism with which he was to dower Puss in Boots.

Perrault was admitted to the Académie Française in 1671. In 1672, against the advice of his influential patron, Colbert, who thought her dowry too low, he married nineteen-year-old Marie Guichon, and they quickly had three children, the youngest of whom, Pierre, has his name on the first editions of *Contes du Temps Passé avec des Moralités*. Perrault was now a very rich bourgeois indeed, as rich as Bluebeard, with a regular and handsome salary as controller-general of the department of public works. But Madame Perrault was to die of smallpox in 1678 and the death of Colbert in 1683 ended Perrault's official career.

An enthusiastic and loving father, he spent his retirement attending to his children's education, besides writing lives of the saints and little comedies, composing his own autobiography and defending the Moderns against the Ancients in the Battle of the Books, that reverberating argument about the relevance of classical literature that shook late seventeenth-century literary life. To this battle, Perrault contributed a four-volume work, *Parallèle des Anciens et des Modernes*, published between 1688 and 1696. He died in 1703. His last book was called: *Éloges des Hommes Illustres du Siècle de Louis XIV*, two volumes, in folio, with a hundred and two portraits.

He also occupied his long retirement by tinkering with the tales that he probably first found in the popular form of the blue paper–covered chap-books called *La Bibliothèque Bleue*. His first attempt was in verse and derived, via the chap-book renderings, from Boccaccio, a version of: "The Marquise de

Salusses, or the Patience of Griselda." The style is that of La Fontaine and the subject matter the abuse of his wife by a psychopathic aristocrat. (I have not included a translation of it here because it is neither a popular tale nor a folk tale, clearly bearing the marks of its derivation, virtually a versified translation of Boccaccio.)

After this first attempt, Perrault published a verse version of the traditional tale "The Ridiculous Wishes" in a society paper, *Le Mercure Galant,* in 1693, and then brought out a collection of these two tales, together with a version of the well-known story "Donkey-Skin," in a little volume in 1694. Strangely enough, this literary exercise sparked off a storm of controversy, including a polished insult from the great pedant and classicist Boileau, who suggested that the donkey-skin more properly belonged to Perrault himself.

Perrault fought back in a sprightly fashion, claiming (in the *Parallèle des Anciens et des Modernes*) that the true inheritors of Boileau's classic Homer were those who delighted in fancies such as ogres with seven-league boots.

Besides, he added in the preface to the second edition of his verse tales, published in 1695, what pleasure fairy tales give to children!

But perhaps the controversy surrounding his verse tales made him think twice before he published his own tales in prose and he put to them, not his own name, but that of his son Pierre Darmancour. Now, his son would have been nineteen when the tales first appeared and was to become a soldier, showing no sign of literary inclinations all the rest of his life. It seems possible that Pierre had first heard these nursery tales from his own nurse and retold them to his interested and indulgent father, perhaps had even noted them down as a schoolroom exercise, and Perrault senior remembered them when he found his own interest in popular literature growing. Nevertheless, whatever kind of literary partnership may have existed between father and son, or father, son and domestic servants, the tales as they exist and were first published in the collection titled *Histoires ou Contes du Temps Passé avec des Moralités* in 1697 bear all the marks of a sophisticated hand and, since the earliest editions, have always been ascribed to Charles Perrault, not the least on the grounds of his known interest in the form.

The style in which these familiar, popular themes were re-created suited them so well that Perrault's versions of the seven stories became the standard ones and, through translation and continuous reprintings and retellings, entered back again into the oral tradition of most European countries, especially that of England. My own grandmother used to tell me the story of "Red Riding Hood" in almost Perrault's very words, although she never spoke one single word of French in all her life. She liked, especially, to pounce on me, roaring, in personation of the wolf's pounce on Red Riding Hood at the end of the story, although she could not have known that Perrault himself suggests this acting-out of the story to the narrator in a note in the margin of the manuscript.

There was a great vogue for fairy tales at the court of Louis XIV, a vogue that grew to ornate, baroque and sometimes monstrous excesses in the later eighteenth century. The stories, as Andrew Lang says, were probably "welcomed in that spirit of sham simplicity which served Louis XIV and his nobles and ladies to appear in Ballets as shepherds and shepherdesses". Though the extravagance of the court was legendary, it was a time of great hardship for the people of France, of constant famine and continuous economic instability. The countryside was still locked in the middle ages and an illiterate peasantry remained rich, if nothing else, in a folk-lore of songs, tales, ceremonies and dances which arrived in elegant magazines after suffering, sometimes, the most extravagant of sea-changes.

Ladies and gentlemen of rank and fortune composed new stories out of magic, traditional elements. There is Madame d'Aulnoy, of whose prolific output "The White Cat," with its handsome prince, magic castle and princess suffering the most exquisite feline transformation, is often mistaken for one of Perrault's and published as such. Le Chevalier Jean de Mailly published his *Illustres Fées, contes galants dediés aux Dames,* in 1698, his *Nouveau recueil des contes des fées* twenty-three years later in 1721. Antoine Galland's translation of the a "Thousand and One Nights" belongs to the early years of the eighteenth century. The fairy tales and tales of wonder became increasingly adult and literary forms; in the hands of Voltaire, the fairy tale turns into an anti-fairy tale—"Candide." Another energetic writer of fairy tales, Madame Leprince de Beaumont, published "Beauty and the Beast," another story often assumed incorrectly to be part of Perrault's legacy, in 1756. As late as 1789, there appeared a massive anthology of fairy tales in forty-one volumes—*Le Cabinet des Fées, ou collection choisie des contes des fées, et autres contes merveilleux,* edited by Charles-Joseph de Mayer.

The fashion terminated abruptly with the French Revolution.

Perrault's tales are told with a great deal of literary art but it is the kind that conceals art; unlike those of many of his contemporaries and successors, his are never artful. His tales retain the simplicity of form and the narrative directness of the country story-teller. His fairies do not have pretty-pretty, invented names like Merluche, Fleur d'Amour and Belle de Nuit; with the sole exception of the Lilac Fairy in "Donkey-Skin," an early story written in a more exotic style than the later ones, his fairies have no names at all because they do not need them. His princes and princesses rarely have names either; the technique of the folk tale demands they exist, in some degree, as abstractions. Red Riding Hood, Hop o' my Thumb, Cinderella and Bluebeard are all descriptions rather than names, nicknames that tell you what a person is rather than who he is. The folk tale tends to define identity by role. Perrault resisted all temptations to the affectation that misses the point of the fairy tale. Madame d'Aulnoy, who did not, could unblushingly name a princess "Belle Etoile" and a prince, "Chéri"; it would have been impossible for Perrault's taste, common sense, and, perhaps, sense of fidelity to his sources to have done so.

Yet the details of his stories—the courtyards paved with marble, the Swiss guards, the gilded chambers, the mirrored corridors, the superbly elegant clothes—are those of Perrault's own world, the sumptuous court of the Sun-King, to whose niece, Elisabeth d'Orléans, the book was originally dedicated.

The earliest European story book to include fairy tales was Straparola's collection of jokes and stories, *La Piacevoli Notte*

(The Delightful Nights), published in Venice between 1550 and 1553, and some of the stories retold by Perrault exist in versions here. Almost all the fifty tales in Giambattista Basile's *Lo Cunto di li cunti* (The Tale of Tales), now usually known as *Il Pentamerone*, published between 1634 and 1636, are fairy tales and many are closely related to Perrault's versions, although Basile wrote and published in an obscure Neapolitan dialect and there seems to have been no direct influence.

Perrault's sources stemmed from the lore of the same kind of country people who told stories to Jacob and Wilhelm Grimm in Germany a hundred years later but, though he retained the narrative form, the simplicity and directness of the folk tale, he extensively rewrote and even, on occasion, censored his sources. The sleeping beauty of Straparola, for example, is impregnated and conceives during her sleep; but Perrault's prince is far too much of a gentleman to take such gross advantage of her. Indeed, he does not even presume to kiss her. And so you will find very little of the savagery and wonder and dark poetry of Grimms' "Household Tales" in Perrault's elegant, witty and sensible pages.

Each century tends to create or re-create fairy tales after its own taste. The Grimms were of the romantic period, the age of Goethe and Schiller; the marvellous excited them, and excited the poets who read them still more. But Perrault, though of an earlier period, was a man who self-consciously defined himself as "modern," who disliked superstition and did not indulge in excesses of the imagination for the imagination's own sake. He was a man who wanted to make of Paris a modern Rome, a visible capital of sweet reason, and his fairy tales are in a style that prefigures the age of enlightenment—a style marked by concision of narrative (there is not an ounce of flab on any story); precision of language; irony; and realism.

Especially in the moral tags at the end of each tale he seems concerned in turning the fairy tales into little parables of experience from which children can learn, without half the pain that Cinderella or Red Riding Hood endured, the way of the world and how to come to no harm in it. The book is intended for children but these children are seen as apprentice adults and the succinct brutality of the traditional tale is modified by the application of rationality.

The wolf consumes Red Riding Hood; what else can you expect if you talk to strange men, comments Perrault briskly. Let's not bother our heads with the mysteries of sado-masochistic attraction. We must learn to cope with the world before we can interpret it. Modern savants with a psycho-analytic bent tend to ignore or berate Perrault because he incorporates certain troubling and intransigent images into a well-mannered schema of good sense, so that they cease to be troubling at all. For example, he seems so appalled by the bloodthirsty antics of Bluebeard that he adds a comforting footnote: no modern husband would behave like this! The consolations he offers are not those of fantasy and the dream but of worldly security seen as such. Bluebeard's wife will use her inheritance to secure for herself another, better husband. The prince in "The Fairies" perceives immediately that a beautiful beggar girl who salivates diamonds is a more auspicious match than any princess. Cinderella forgives her sisters and even finds them husbands; and Perrault is humane enough to have made them, not ugly, a condition that cannot in itself be cured (although—vide "Ricky with the Tuft"—the perception of ugliness may be changed), but proud, a moral defect that may be rectified by a moral effort.

Even Perrault's specifically magical beings, the Lilac Fairy, Cinderella's godmother and the guests at the Sleeping Beauty's christening, have rather less the air of supernatural beings derived from pagan legend about them than that of women of independent means who've done quite well for themselves, one way and another, and are prepared to help along a little sister who finds herself in difficulties, personages as worldly-wise and self-confident as Mae West.

Perrault's consummate craftsmanship and his good-natured cynicism (and "Puss in Boots," or the Cat as Con Man, is a masterpiece of benevolent cynicism) are not qualities much present in twentieth-century children's literature, which tends to concentrate on the nourishing of a rich, imaginative life. But perhaps the very need for a rich imaginative life is an indication that the circumstances of real life are unsatisfactory.

From the work of this humane, tolerant and kind-hearted Frenchman, children can learn enlightened self-interest from Puss; resourcefulness and courage from Hop o' my Thumb; the advantages of patronage from Cinderella; the benefits of long engagements from the Sleeping Beauty; the dangers of heedlessness from Red Riding Hood; and gain much pleasure, besides.

To the stories from *Histoires ou Contes du Temps Passé avec des Moralités,* I have added prose translations of the two tales in verse, "The Foolish Wishes" and "Donkey-Skin."